A Kayla

Wolves in Sheep's Clothing

*Enjoy,
Amy C. Laundrie*

by
Amy C. Laundrie

Royal Fireworks Press
Unionville, New York

To my husband, Frank, who, while trapped on long car rides, gives helpful critiques of my manuscripts. May we travel many more miles together.

Acknowledgments

Thanks to my agent, Jane Johnson, whose dedication, compassion and charm bring joy to all.

For their patient help with research, my thanks to Dr. Westphal, Marion Moran, Officer Anderson, Maggie MacDonald, Dennis Prusik, John Jacobs, Melanie Faivre, Bill and Bev Gaedke, and Donovan Keeble.

For their critical eye, sincere appreciation goes to Gayle Rosengren, Julia Pferdehirt, Kathleen Ernst, Eileen Daily, Gisela Hamm, Patricia Zettner, Sharon Dricken, Marjorie Berg, Kiki Laundrie, David Fugina and Patricia Notes. Thanks to Heather Laundrie who inspired the adventurous horse scenes and to Heidi Laundrie who invoked the humorous and warmhearted moments.

Copyright © 2001, R Fireworks Publishing Co., Ltd.
All Rights Reserved.

Royal Fireworks Press
First Avenue, PO Box 399
Unionville, NY 10988-0399
(845) 726-4444
FAX: (845) 726-3824
email: rfpress@frontiernet.net

ISBN: 0-88092-549-3

Printed in the United States of America on acid-free, recycled paper using vegetable-based inks by the Royal Fireworks Printing Co. of Unionville, New York.

CHAPTER 1

The Face in the Window

Kayla Montgomery was lost and frightened. The unpredictable *whaa-ooo* sound of gusting wind, the *splosh* of falling snow on lower branches and the *rush, rush* of last year's oak leaves as animals prowled about didn't help her nerves. The woods seemed alive. She tightened her grip on the reins. Her horse, Sundance, was nervous too, flicking her ears back and forth, probably wondering why she wasn't back in Aunt Maggie's barn where Kayla kept her.

Kayla had planned this long trail ride to keep both their minds off missing Fortune, the racehorse that had become Sundance's best buddy and Kayla's second love. Fortune had gone to a loving family, but the loss was still difficult.

Kayla reached down and petted Sundance on the neck. "I guess we shouldn't have taken that new path." She shaded her eyes and looked upward to a ridge. "Let's try going this way. If this doesn't work, we'll have to follow our tracks all the way back."

As they climbed, Kayla forgot her worry for a moment. It was such a gorgeous day, one with a breath of spring. If her boyfriend Rob had come along, his artistic eye would have appreciated the early afternoon patterns of shadows in the snow: heavy, stark trunk and branch shadows contrasted with softer leaf and pine needle shadows.

Kayla grinned wryly. He might also have found their way back!

Kayla signaled Sundance to trot up the rest of the hill. Everything around her was unfamiliar. *That twisted cedar resembles a grizzly bear, and look how vivid that clump of red dogwood is against the snow. Over there is a fallen tree whose many branches are arched like octopus' arms.* This new scenery would be worth the worry of getting lost if only she could find a path leading back to the road. She breathed in the pristine air, then sighed. Sometimes her passion for adventure got her into difficulties that were hard to escape.

They turned a bend and were headed down an unfamiliar straight stretch of ridge when—*Woof! woof! woof!* Kayla pulled back on the reins and peered through the woods, seeing dogs in a pen next to a forest green house. She debated. *Should I ask for directions at the house rather than backtrack all the way home?* A snowmobile trail leading to the back yard answered her question.

As they turned onto the snowmobile trail, Kayla studied the two menacing dogs. Rottweilers, she guessed, were barking and lunging at their pen door. The back door of the house opened and a round-faced man, about her grandfather's age, stocky, tall and dressed in overalls and red plaid, appeared. He yelled, "This is private property! Get the hell out of here, or I'll let my dogs loose!"

What's his problem? Kayla thought, as much startled as scared. First his dogs barked threateningly at her, and now he yelled at her to get off his property. She tried to quiet Sundance and turn her around, but she wasn't fast enough to suit this nervous old man.

"Get going! Now!" he screamed.

Kayla waved in an all-right-I'm-leaving gesture. As she and Sundance turned, a flash of light from a picture window drew her eye. A white-haired woman held a hand mirror and was tilting it back and forth so the light hit Kayla. *Is she signaling me?* When she lowered the mirror, sunlight glinted on metal. *A wheelchair?* With her face wrinkled in distress, the old woman was trying to say something. She was mouthing the words *Help me!*

Did the woman have to stay alone with this yelling man? Was he abusing her?

"I warned you!" the man shouted.

Hadn't he seen my surrender gesture? Too late, Kayla realized he had let the dogs loose.

Gr-rrrrr! Woof! Woof! They *were* Rottweilers, and they were charging straight at her. Adrenalin pumping, Kayla reined Sundance all the way around. "Go—Go!" she shouted, kicking hard. The mare leaped into a gallop, raced down the snowmobile trail and onto the straightaway. Still the Rottweilers were closing as Kayla and Sundance rounded the bend. The steep, snow-covered hill was just ahead, and with Sundance's metal shoes, they'd tumble down for sure at this speed. When they reached the crown of the hill, Kayla reined Sundance down to a jog. "Easy, girl." Kayla's voice quivered. The dogs' barking told her they were just lunges away.

At the bottom of the hill, Kayla looked back. The dogs crested the slope, charging toward them. In seconds, they had Kayla and Sundance between them. Her head spinning, almost reeling from shock, Kayla watched as the bigger of the two dogs rushed in and attacked her horse's legs. It meant to sever a tendon!

"No!" Kayla screamed.

CHAPTER 2

Rottweiler

Sundance tripped, pitching Kayla forward. The mare regained her footing, and when the dog attacked again, Sundance's powerful hoof caught the side of its head, sending it flying into the brush. Now the second Rottweiler lunged forward and clamped its teeth down on Sundance's foreleg.

"Get!" Kayla screamed. Sundance was being slashed and all she could do was shout. If she jumped off, they'd attack her, too. Even if she could grab a stick, she wouldn't be able to defend herself against these killers.

The mare squealed and reared back on her hind legs. Kayla grabbed her mane just in time to hang on. Sundance shook her foreleg violently and threw the smaller dog off. As soon as Sundance landed, the bigger dog, now recovered and waiting for its opening, sprang for the mare's throat. Kayla kicked her leg forward, meeting the beast with the toe of her boot, just inches from Sundance's neck. Stunned, the bigger Rottweiler still had fight left. It lunged again. *Bam!* This time Kayla put her hip into her kick, and her boot heel nailed the dog in the nose. It landed, yelping.

Kayla didn't have to signal Sundance to move. The mare tore off with every ounce of her strength, back the way they had come. Kayla looked back. Both dogs were on their feet, their ears were down, and they looked defeated. A whistle sounded. The man was calling his dogs back.

When Kayla was sure the dogs weren't following, she brought Sundance to a halt. She jumped down to check Sundance's bleeding left foreleg. Kayla wasn't sure if wrapping her scarf around the wound would introduce infection or prevent it. Since the foreleg wasn't bleeding badly, she concentrated on retracing their tracks and finding their way home. *If only we weren't so far away!*

It was dusk by the time Kayla reached Aunt Maggie's farm. "Aunt Maggie!" she yelled as soon as she neared the farmhouse. Her aunt's face appeared at the window. "I need help!" Kayla yelled. Aunt Maggie hurried out. "Sundance was attacked—two Rottweilers." She pointed to the blood-streaked leg.

Aunt Maggie was already examining the slash marks. "I'll call the vet." She was almost to the door when she turned back. "Were these stray dogs?"

"No, they belonged to some man who turned them loose on us."

Aunt Maggie blinked in surprise, but she quickly recovered. "I'll call the police, too." The urgency in her voice and the word *police* set Kayla's heart racing once again. "Put her in the cross ties," Aunt Maggie yelled back.

Kayla led Sundance to the barn. Her heart ached as she exchanged the saddle and bridle for a halter and snapped Sundance in the cross ties. The mare had gone through so much: being foundered when her previous owner had carelessly allowed her to get to the grain bin and eat until she was sick, and soon after—well, Kayla didn't want to think about what Vern Schaffner had done. Now this.

Aunt Maggie hurried back with a bucket of warm water and antiseptic. "Doc Kelley's on another call, but she'll come as soon as she can. The police will be over to question you. Now let's see what we've got here."

Aunt Maggie was gentle, but Sundance's ears drooped, and her skin twitched in pain.

Aunt Maggie asked, "What happened?"

Kayla hung her head. How she wished she hadn't tried that new path. "At the deer stand I took a different way that led up to a ridge. I didn't see any 'No Trespassing' signs, but I might have missed them." Kayla remembered how she'd been enjoying the shadow patterns then. "We were on top of the ridge when I heard some dogs barking. A man yelled for me to get off his property. When I turned to go, a flash of light caught my eye. A woman in a wheelchair was at a picture window, signaling me. I think she was mouthing the words 'help me'."

Aunt Maggie dropped the rag in the soapy water and stood up. "Help me?"

"Yes, and she had a pained expression. Desperate, actually. I was looking at her, when the man let the dogs loose. They charged. They... they caught us at the bottom of the hill. Is Sundance going to be all right?"

"One wound is deep, but it's not as bad as I first thought. Doc will fix her up. I left Ashley in the playpen so I need to check on her. Come on in if you want."

"No, I'll wait here with Sundance for the police."

A few minutes later, an unfamiliar police officer stepped out of a squad car. He was short and had a marine haircut.

"Isn't Officer Finley available?" *Right,* Kayla told herself. *Big mouth. Sound rude and ungrateful. Great way to make this guy's acquaintance!*

"He has the day off. Are you Kayla Montgomery?"

"Yes."

"I'm Officer Bork. Tell me what happened."

While Kayla told the story of the attack, Officer Bork took notes. "Let me take a look at the horse." Kayla brought Sundance out under the barn light, and Bork studied her leg. "Is that the only injury?" *What? Did he want more?* Kayla fought against being sarcastic. She needed this man's help. "That's the worst one, she answered."

"I have to level with you, Miss Montgomery. We'll need to check out the property lines. If you were trespassing, you don't have much of a case."

"I'm not interested in suing him, if that's what you're getting at, but I don't want other people to get attacked, or for him to get away with this. Isn't there a law against siccing attack dogs on people even if they're trespassing?"

"Dogs in rural areas are allowed to run free; however, they must remain on their property. My guess is they never left their land. The property owner could insist we give you a citation for trespassing. Now, if these dogs should have a history of attacking people, and I'll check that out, too, you'd have a case against the property owner."

"I'm most concerned about what I saw just before the attack." After Kayla told him about the old woman, she asked, "Can you check that out?"

"Yes. We'll contact the woman. If she isn't being taken care of, or if she is living in poor conditions, we'll ask Social Services to investigate."

"All right. Will you please let me know what you find?"

"I will. I'll also need to make sure the dogs have had their rabies shots."

Rabies! Kayla had never thought to worry about that.

The officer must have seen her blanch. "I'm sure they've had them," he answered quickly.

As soon as the officer left, Kayla went inside. Aunt Maggie had her hands full with eleven-month-old Ashley, whose usual pattern of stagger, crash, cry, then back up and staggering again, was exhausting. Kayla recalled Aunt Maggie once saying, she was going to market a crash helmet for toddlers. "What did the officer say, Kayla?"

"That he'll check that the dogs have had their shots and that I'm in as much trouble for trespassing as the man is for siccing his attack dogs on me." Kayla shook her head. "Someone will go out there and talk to the woman, though. Then we'll know if she really needs help."

"I'll do a bit of investigating myself," Aunt Maggie said. "I'll call our friend Todd Gillespie this evening. He lives in the yellow house near where this happened and he might have some answers." Aunt Maggie sighed. "I wish Jim were here."

"Have you heard from him?"

"Yes. The flight to Russia went smoothly, and the crane eggs arrived safely." Kayla knew how nervous he'd been. As a ranger for Nicolet National Forest, he'd been selected to accompany the rare Siberian crane eggs (which were due to hatch shortly) to a perservation project in Russia. "It's going to be a long two weeks," Aunt Maggie continued. "They want him to make sure the chicks are developing on schedule."

"Speaking of schedules," Kayla said, glancing at her watch, "I'd better call to see if Josie will take notes for my Native American culture class."

"Sure," her friend said a few minutes later. "What's up?"

After Kayla told Josie the story, she almost wished she hadn't. Josie was wild with accusations against the dog owner and Officer Bork. "You need to go to class," Kayla finally said. "We'll talk later. Besides, I just heard a car pull in. I hope it's Doc Kelley."

It was. Doc Kelley complimented Aunt Maggie on the thoroughness of her wound cleansing, then she stitched up the deepest cut. "Give Sundance these pain pills and antibiotics. No hard riding for a while, and call me if the swelling persists or there are new symptoms." She looked at Kayla. "I doubt I need to warn you about going out there again."

Kayla shook her head, but the face in the window haunted her while she drove home. She changed clothes, shedding the old fleece pants for jeans and a lavender sweater. As she brushed her hair, she heard Mom's car pull in. *Darn.* She'd hoped to avoid what was coming.

"Aren't you late for class?" Mom asked, as Kayla pulled a jacket out of the closet.

Kayla said, "Yes. Josie's taking notes for me, but if I hurry I'll make tonight's history class."

"Did something happen?" Mom stood in front of the door. She wasn't about to let Kayla go without an explanation. Kayla tried not to notice her mom's worry lines. The lines and the silver hair had appeared at the same time. Both came a year and a half ago, shortly after the car Kayla had been driving on icy pavement spun out of control, smashing into a pickup, and killing her brother, Ned.

Kayla gave her mom a watered-down version of the dog attack. Even so, a deep pucker formed between Mom's eyebrows. "You go ahead to class. We can talk about this when you get back."

As Kayla drove, questions and thoughts bounced around in her head. *Is the man with the attack dogs married to the woman who wanted help? Is he abusing her? Had she tried calling the police or Social Services herself? Why is she in a wheelchair?* And finally, *What, if anything, should I do?*

She forced herself to push the questions aside as she opened the door to her history class. Dr. Nerad had already started his lecture. She scurried to a seat in the back. The professor lifted his eyebrows at her, then continued lecturing.

He was rather handsome, Kayla thought, taking in his brown hair, narrow face, and pleasing features. Except for his eyes. They were squinty, mole eyes. Kayla shook her head. She was supposed to be concentrating on taking lecture notes.

Dr. Nerad had the habit of raising the pitch of the final syllable in every sentence. The first day he'd told the class he'd created the speech pattern to hold their attention. It got noticed, that was for sure. As Dr. Nerad ended class, Kayla positioned her pen. *How would one graphically show a rise in pitch?* "Read chapter three by Wednes-DAY!" she wrote. "Midterm counts one-third toward your final gr-AAADE! Also research paper and a fi-NAAAL!"

"You're dismissed," Dr. Nerad said. "Oh, and I'd like to speak to Miss Montgomery after class." Kayla's mouth instantly turned dry. Did he know what she'd been doing? She quickly closed the notebook.

After everyone left, she came forward. "Y-yes, Dr. Nerad?"

"Have a seat, Miss Montgomery. May I call you Kayla?"

"Of course."

"I've been observing you"—Kayla took a deep breath to calm herself—"and I have something to ask."

Questions raced through her mind. He was going to ask if she wanted to pass this course, if she intended on growing up and taking her education seriously, if—

"And," he continued, "I'm impressed with your attitude and sense of responsibility."

Is this a joke? She'd just been doodling his speech patterns in her notebook and she'd been late for class again today. "So, I was wondering if you'd be interested in organizing my office library for me. I must admit things are a mess in there. I had a much larger office at Cornell, and just haven't found the time to sort through which books to store." He looked at her for an uncomfortably long time. "I think you might be just the one to help me out. The college will pay you minimum wage, and I'll put in an extra two dollars per hour."

He was offering her a job! Kayla realized her mouth was hanging open and she closed it discreetly. She quickly figured she'd earn more than she did at the Indian museum and since her hours there had been cut, she could use the money.

"How many hours do you think it would take?" Kayla asked.

"Oh, ten to fifteen."

"And I'd be putting your books in order?"

"That's right. You could choose your own hours. Just work around my office hours."

Being able to schedule the work herself would make it easy to see Rob. "Yes, I think I could do it," she said.

Dr. Nerad grinned. "Very good. Take a look at my office hours posted on the door. Meanwhile I'll try to do some organizing myself and let the history office know you'll be asking for the key."

Dr. Nerad turned his back to her and began shuffling through papers. She must have been dismissed. It suddenly occurred to her he didn't use his professor change-of-pitch voice when he spoke just to her.

Rob was waiting for her outside. Her heart pounded when she saw him. When he was truly happy, his blue eyes sparked and danced, just as they were doing now. "Hi, there," she said, meeting him for a kiss. She missed though, kissing his bristly, reddish-blond moustache instead. They laughed.

Rob delighted her with the mischievous half-smile she'd grown to love. "Try again. You must be out of practice."

After going through a separation in November, they had reunited on New Year's Day. She put her arms around him and their lips met right on target this time.

Rob held Kayla's shoulders and asked, "Did that weird duck keep you after class?"

"Dr. Nerad has his Ph.D. and has published two books. Besides, he's not a duck. I've decided he's a mole."

"Okay, a mole who ought to get some speech therapy."

"Well the mole sure surprised me." Kayla laughed. "I thought he was going to yell at me for being late and then doodling during class. Instead he asked if I wanted a job."

"You didn't take it, did you?"

"It's only temporary, arranging a library for him, and the money's good." Kayla sensed Rob's disapproval. "I can pick my own hours. In fact, do you want to go with me now to copy down his office hours?"

"So, you'll work when he's not around?"

"Yeah." Rob seemed happier with the decision now. "Let's hurry so we can go get a cup of coffee," Kayla said. "I have to tell you what happened while I was out trail riding."

Dr. Nerad's office was on the far end of the second floor. After studying his hours, Kayla left a post-it note on the door saying she'd come on Friday morning. That would give him the week to remove anything he wanted or do some organizing on his own.

"So, tell," Rob said after they were seated at their usual table at Berkley's.

Rob's reaction after her tale was far different from her mother's. Instead of the tired, slumped shoulders, Rob squared his. "Is this guy a maniac?" he almost yelled. "Letting vicious dogs loose to chase you! Did you call the police?"

"Aunt Maggie did, and an officer named Bork came out. I was trespassing though, so basically it's a draw. He could demand that I get a citation, and I could sue him for the vet bill—if I could prove he knew his dogs were vicious." Kayla rubbed her temples. She was getting a headache. She sighed. "I'm really worried about the woman—living with a man like that. I guess we just have to wait to see what the police investigation shows."

Kayla finished her coffee, then said, "I better get back. I want to check on Sundance before it gets too late."

They walked out of the restaurant, the damp March air making Kayla zip up her coat. Rob put his arm around her. "This weekend is supposed to be warmer. I'm planning something special for Friday night. Going to be available?"

"I may be," Kayla teased. "What do you have in mind?"

"All I'll tell you is that you'll need warm clothes and a swim suit. A bikini would be nice."

"I don't own a bikini."

Kayla's smile made him pull her closer. "I may have to get you one."

At their cars, Rob said, "See you later. And please don't do anything reckless. I'd like to keep you around." With a final kiss, he was gone.

As Kayla drove out of the parking lot, she remembered their first kiss. They had been in a marshy area for the sandhill crane count when Rob had lifted off her camouflage

16

hat, freeing her hair. As the shadow of a big bird crossed their path, their lips met. There had been many more kisses since then, but they had stopped when Julius appeared. And again when Liz and finally Luke entered the scene. She and Rob had prevailed, though, his tenderness and mischievous half-smile endearing him to her.

Kayla pulled into Aunt Maggie's driveway, then headed for the barn. Sundance seemed a bit groggy, and Kayla didn't fuss with her long before heading to the farmhouse.

"Did you find out anything, Aunt Maggie?" she asked.

"I called Todd Gillespie. He gave me an earful. Have a seat." They sat at the kitchen table. "I already told some of this to your mom. Their names are Olaf and Daisy Erickson. They moved into that house two years ago. Olaf's a trapper, and he's the one who caused a stir last winter when he set traps in the roadsides. Two of the Gillespie's cats were killed."

Kayla said, "I remember hearing about that."

"Todd went over there to talk to him, and he turned his dogs loose that time, too. Fortunately, Todd made it to his car okay, but unfortunately he never reported it." Aunt Maggie shook her head. "Now he wishes he had."

"So do I," Kayla said. "Maybe Olaf-the-Rottweiler, would have thought twice about doing it again." As she gave him the nickname, she realized even his physical appearance resembled his dogs'—all had short, coarse black hair and stocky builds.

"Yes. So, Todd finally tracked him down at the coffee shop where Olaf meets his trapping buddies. Todd tried to make him understand that he was trapping family pets and how awful it had been when Todd's son discovered the suffering cat. It might have been easier to reason with the guy if he hadn't been surrounded by his pals. He blustered something about his rights, and the next thing you know, the Gillespies lost their second cat. Even two months later Todd is still livid.

"Then Todd made a mistake. He picked up the traps and took them home. He was afraid one of his kids might get caught in one. When Olaf discovered what Todd had done, he called the police. Todd had to pay a huge fine for tampering with licensed traps! Can you believe it? This is one to stay away from, Kayla. We're dealing with a clever man."

A clever and cruel man, Kayla was sure. *Why else would his wife be pleading for help? What kind of a marriage did they have?* It appeared as remote as possible from the kind of sharing, loving relationship she hoped to have someday. A relationship founded on trust and respect. *Olaf must not love Daisy, but did she love him? Why did she stay?* And the final question: *How involved should I get?*

O O O

Kayla's mom met her at the door. "Sorry," Kayla said. "I stopped out to see Sundance and visit with Aunt Maggie and time just slipped away." Aunt Maggie had said she'd spoken to Mom and Dad about Sundance's accident. Kayla hoped they'd been given the G-rated version instead of the PG.

When Dad appeared, Kayla wondered if this would be one of those all-night grilling sessions, but all Dad said was, "You're going to have to be very careful, Kayla. You never know what kind of lunatic this man could turn out to be."

"I will be," she said, noticing how her mother's lower lip trembled.

○ ○ ○

Over the next several days, her parents insisted she tell them exactly where she was going, and she hoped they'd let up soon. Kayla still hadn't heard from the police, so she finally called them. Officer Bork said, "I checked and the dogs are current with their rabies shots."

Kayla let out a long sigh of relief. "So, did you talk to the woman?"

"I visited yesterday. Daisy Erickson was perfectly fine. Her clothes were clean, and they had just had lunch and were listening to a tape of old radio shows."

"Was Mr. Erickson there the whole time you talked to her?"

"Yes, he was."

"But what if she was afraid to say something in front of him?"

"I didn't see a problem," the officer insisted. "If you do have some hard and fast evidence of abuse, give me a call back."

Kayla shook her head. She suspected that if she'd reported a child in distress, the police would have taken it much more seriously. Was Mrs. Erickson less important because she was elderly, or because they expected her to have the means to help herself? Kayla wasn't sure Mrs. Erickson had those means. She decided to call Todd Gillespie herself.

"Olaf is capable of just about anything," Todd said later that afternoon when she reached him. "I'm afraid he's going to show up at my house someday with a shotgun. We never used to lock our doors during the day. Now we do, and we even bought a security system. Last month my wife ran into the Ericksons at the hardware store. She was going to say hello to Daisy, but the man walked between them. He wouldn't let her talk to his wife. I wouldn't be a bit surprised if he was abusing his wife, but I'm sure not going to get involved again. One hefty fine is enough."

Hey, Kayla thought after thanking Todd and saying good-bye, *the Rottweiler could sue me for trespassing and take every penny I have in the bank. He'd be lucky to get a meal at McDonald's.*

Kayla tried to put the old woman out of her thoughts, but her mind kept whirring. She could write Mrs. Erickson a note and include her number in case it was needed, but what if Mr. Erickson read it and found out? *If only I knew when he would be out of the house. It would be better if I could speak to Mrs. Erickson in person.*

Todd Gillespie had gone to see Daisy's husband at the coffee house where he met his trapping buddies. Did Rottweiler still go there? If she found out when, she might be able to meet with Mrs. Erickson during that time. She'd call Todd and find out. *No,* she decided, *it'd be better to call The Corner Cafe. They might know if there was a certain time the trappers met.*

The woman who answered the telephone said, "Dead-man Olaf? Sure, I know him."

"Dead-man Olaf?" Kayla asked, a shiver going up her spine.

The woman laughed. "That's what his trapping buddies call him. He's lost a couple of friends, and since they both happened to be stocky like Olaf, their widows gave him their husbands' clothes, which he wears. His friends have fun with him, guessing whose clothes he's wearing. But, what can I help you with?"

"I was wondering when he comes in."

"Thursday and Saturday afternoon at four o'clock. Leaves at six-thirty. He and the other guys have been at it for years."

Kayla's pulse raced. "Thank you." After hanging up, she wrapped her arms tightly around herself. She'd go tomorrow, Thursday night.

Shortly after, her mother came home from her job as an aide for students with special needs. "Kayla," she said, "something important has come up. Could we sit and talk?"

Kayla's heart hammered. Mom looked serious. "What's up?" She kept her voice light, hoping it would somehow ease what Mom had to say.

"It's Joey."

Since he had moved into the school district in January, Kayla had heard a lot about Joey. She thought of him as the kid who once threw a desk at another boy, cussed out the principal, brought in a switchblade, and chronically had head lice. He'd been suspended twice in the past two months. "What happened this time?"

"This time something was done to him." It took several seconds before Mom could continue and her voice was quavery. "Today when I was listening to him read a story, his eyes welled up with tears." Mom's own eyes turned misty. "His grandmother was taken to the hospital last night. They think it was a stroke."

"He was living with his grandma, wasn't he?"

Mom nodded. "She's the only stable person in his life. Since she took him in, he's been coming to school regularly and his behavior's improved, too." Mom sighed. "His father is dead, and his mother is in jail. Her drinking and drug habits are out of control, and he talks about the different men she brought home. I hope he never has to live with her again." Mom continued. "But here's what I wanted to talk to you about. Dad and I spoke to his social worker and offered to let him stay here tonight. He'll be staying with a foster family while his grandma recuperates, and they come back from vacation tomorrow. Is that all right?"

"Sure, it's fine with me."

Mom sighed again. "I wish I didn't get so close to these kids. It almost broke my heart when Johnny moved last month, and last year it was Sarah." She shook her head. "Joey is the worst, though. I can't distance myself from him. Maybe it's because he's so vulnerable."

Kayla was at a loss to know what to say. Her mother had her own Daisy Erickson. When Dad opened the door, Mom said, "He'll be coming tonight after supper. Would you help me get N-Ned's room ready?"

"He's staying in Ned's room?" Suddenly, Kayla's stomach lurched.

"Yes," Mom said. "It seems silly to pull out the sleeper couch when he can use the extra bedroom."

The extra bedroom? Is that what Ned's memory has been reduced to? It has only been a year and a half, and now someone else will be sleeping in his room, pawing through his things. Kayla suddenly was shrouded in shame. Surely this boy could stay in Ned's room for one night. As Kayla helped her mother put sheets on the bed, neither talked, and Kayla guessed her mother didn't trust her voice. Cleaning Ned's troom had to be very difficult for her mother.

Later, Kayla tried to work on her paper for Native American studies, but her mind kept drifting, and when the doorbell rang, she jumped. Soon, a young boy's boisterous voice announced, "Hey, do you got any good video games?"

"No," Dad said, "but there's a basketball hoop and a bike."

"No Nintendo 64?"

"'Fraid not," Dad said. "I do have a flying model plane, though. It's too dark tonight, but maybe we can fly it another time."

Another time? Kayla wondered. *Maybe they are planning on doing this again.*

"Do you want to see where you're sleeping?" Mom asked.

"Sure," Joey answered. Kayla could hear his loud, stomping feet.

"This is the dead boy's room, isn't it?"

There was a long pause. *How dare he?* Kayla wanted to run out of her bedroom and shake him. Then she remembered what his life must be like with no father, a messed-up mother and sick grandma. She got up and headed toward the voices.

"This was our son Ned's room," Mom said, her voice cracking a bit.

"I heard your daughter was driving the car when he got killed," Joey said bluntly. "Is that right?"

Kayla's knees swayed and she clutched the doorjamb. She didn't need this right now. Not with all the worry about Daisy. The strain in her muscles grew tighter until she took several deep breaths. When she finally had her emotions under control, she walked down the hall to meet the boy.

Mom glanced apologetically at Kayla then said, "Joey, this is our daughter Kayla. Kayla, Joey." Kayla took in the messy brown hair, big brown eyes, and crooked teeth.

"I still got a mother," Joey blurted out to everyone. "And I got a seventeen-year-old sister living in Arizona."

"Oh," Mom said, "she's close to Kayla's age."

"Tiffani has a convertible," Joey bragged, "and she's saving to get an even better car."

Mom nodded, then said, "We were just going to tour the rest of the house before starting on Joey's homework. Come join us, Kayla."

Kayla tagged along, but the comments were overshadowed by Joey's words still echoing in her head: *sister was driving the car; sister was driving the car.* When Dad said he'd help Joey with his math assignment, Kayla took the opportunity to escape. "I better get to my books, too."

Not long after, Mom said, "All right, you two. It's time for Joey to get to bed. School day tomorrow."

Kayla waited until he was in his pajamas, and she'd heard him ask for a night light. Then she joined them. "Just wanted to say good-night," she said.

"I only need the night light on so I know how to get to the bathroom," he said so quickly Kayla knew he was embarrassed. "And I like to keep the door closed." *Had he reason to be afraid of the night?* Kayla's stomach lurched to think he probably had.

"Good-night," Mom said, bending down and stroking his hair. "See you in the morning." She closed the bedroom door, and the three of them stood staring at it a moment. Kayla's thoughts were so jumbled she couldn't sort them out enough to talk. Her dad also looked too full of emotion and simply reached for Mom, then Kayla. The three of them stood huddled together. Kayla's mind kept repeating the unbelievable: *Another boy is sleeping in Ned's bed tonight.*

In the morning, Kayla awoke to hear the shower. Soon Mom said, "Joey, time for breakfast."

Kayla stumbled out of bed and headed to the bathroom. When she opened the door, steam poured out. She backed away. Joey hadn't turned on the ventilation fan. Closing her eyes, she dashed in, turned the dial, then dashed back to her room. *Steam!* Would she ever get over this crazy phobia she had with steam? It seemed so silly. She forced herself to go back into the bathroom, but it was so much like the heat pouring from the scalding bathtub faucet when she'd accidentally turned it on as a youngster that her heart pounded fiercely and she backed out again. *Scalding water, slippery bubbles, trying to get out...to get out.* Kayla shook her head. She'd forget the shower for now and just dress for the farm.

When she was ready, she walked into the kitchen in time to see Joey licking jam off his butter knife. He stared at her. "Hi," she said in a tone that didn't encourage a response.

"Good morning," Mom said. "Do you want some toast?"

"I need to head to Aunt Maggie's. I'll get something later."

Kayla was about to say good-bye to Joey when he narrowed his eyes at her. "I won't need to stay here no more. My grandma's getting out of the hospital."

Kayla met her mother's eyes and knew this wasn't necessarily true. "I hope so," Kayla said. "I'm off, but you two have a good day at school."

"Drive carefully," Mom said as Kayla headed out the door. "We're supposed to get four inches of snow, and it's already starting."

Slippery roads. Just like that day she was taking Ned to his dental appointment and the car spun out of control. Nothing could undo that terrible day, though, and she forced herself to concentrate on Daisy instead. Would the snow make it difficult to get to her house?

While Kayla cared for Sundance, went to class, then shoveled the sidewalk and driveway, her mind worked on more questions. *When I get to the Erickson house, will*

Mrs. Erickson let me in? Should I just come right out and ask if Mrs. Erickson needs help? What if Rottweiler comes home early and discovers me?

At four-thirty, Kayla wrote her parents a note. "I'll be home around seven." They were used to her hastily scrawled notes so maybe they wouldn't wonder. Kayla hated to be so evasive, but if she told them her true plans, they'd never let her go.

Snow blew as she headed to the car. Finding the Erickson house again on horseback would be hard enough, but finding it by road would be even worse. She searched back roads for half an hour and never found a green house. At an intersection, she decided to turn right on the winding road for her final try. Shortly after her headlights caught snowmobile tracks. Olaf Erickson's? When the tracks took yet another fork, she followed them. There weren't any houses for a long stretch, then another road intersected to the right. The tracks came from that direction. She turned in. As she rounded a corner, a Dead End sign glared at her. It looked as if there was a house just ahead. Its driveway wasn't plowed, but she turned in anyway. Two dogs barked ferociously and lunged at the fence. Kayla recognized the forest green house. She'd found Daisy Erickson.

CHAPTER 3

Who-whoo?

She parked behind a yellow, older model Cadillac in the driveway. The unshoveled front walk seemed to serve as a warning to stay away. The drapes were drawn, but light shone through. A set of tracks coming from the back door reassured Kayla that Rottweiler had left. Did she dare go in for just a few minutes? The drapes moved. Kayla glanced at her watch. Twenty minutes and she should be back in her car. The drapes opened a bit more and Mrs. Erickson's frantic eyes peered out. She looked like a trapped mouse in a wolf's den. Kayla tried to appear non-threatening and smiled as she approached the house. Mrs. Erickson's eyebrows arched, and she opened the window.

"Hello, Mrs. Erickson," Kayla said gently. "My name is Kayla Montgomery. I'm the person who was riding the horse past here a few days ago."

Daisy Erickson squinted through her glasses. "Horse?"

"Yes. I thought you were trying to tell me something. You had a mirror—"

"Oh, yes, my mother's tortoise-shell mirror." Kayla heard the whir of the older woman's chair as she wheeled over and unlocked the door. "Come on in."

Kayla stepped in. Even though the house was warm, Mrs. Erickson wore a blue coat. She was even more frail looking than Kayla had first thought, and her voice was equally fragile and childlike. "My mother gave me that mirror when I turned twenty-one, the year before I married Olaf."

Kayla nodded.

"Come sit down."

Daisy wheeled over to the end table where a cigarette burned. She took a puff. The room smelled of stale smoke and of being shut up all winter. Kayla took in the embroidered doilies on dressers and the crocheted afghan on the couch before finally noticing the filled ashtrays. Phew! This place needed a good cleaning and airing out.

"What did you say your name was?"

"Kayla. Kayla Montgomery."

"Good to meet you. Call me Daisy." Daisy suddenly frowned. "Rip and Trucker stopped barking?"

"Rip and Trucker? Oh, the dogs. Yes, I don't hear them any more."

"Olaf's dogs," Daisy mused. "He got them when the neighbor started walking through our back yard."

"I see."

"You'd better go now."

Kayla blinked. "I... I just wanted to make sure you were all right, that you didn't need anything."

"You better go now," she repeated.

Kayla felt foolish. Had she misinterpreted the woman's "help me" message?

Daisy suddenly asked, "Did you ride your horse here?"

"No."

"Oh, I wish I could ride a horse again. I was a champion rider in my time."

"Really?"

Daisy nodded. "When I was eighteen, I won the grand championship for jumping at the state show."

"I like to jump, too."

"Tell me what you like about jumping."

It struck Kayla that Daisy was starved for attention. "What I like most about jumping," she began, "is the communication with the horse. I remember taking Sundance over a long cross-country course. I was nervous because I wasn't sure how she would react to strange jumps, but we made it over the stone wall, the pile of tires, and the scary blue tarp. Then we had to enter the woods and go up a hill. The jump came quickly, and I wasn't prepared. I didn't signal Sundance with my legs, and by all rights, she shouldn't have gone over, but she did anyway. It was then I realized she was trying her best and meant to make it a clear round. The tenth jump was also uphill, and Sundance was getting tired. I signaled her with my legs, a we-can-do-this kind of squeeze, and she gave the extra burst of energy. We cleared it and went on to finish the course. A perfect round. She and I worked like a team that day. We knew what each other was thinking. Does that sound unbelievable to you?"

"No." Daisy shook her head. "I know what you mean." Then, suddenly, she repeated, "You better go now."

"All right," Kayla said, wondering at the quick mood swings. "It was good talking to you, and I'm glad to know everything's all right."

Kayla walked to the door and had her hand on the knob when Daisy blurted out, "He pinches me. Hard!" Daisy held out her arm revealing a purplish bruise. "He gets mad, and he grabs me hard and the only reason I wet my pants is because he doesn't take me to the bathroom in time. It isn't my fault. It isn't my fault."

Daisy's face had been like a two-way mirror, showing only what Daisy wanted Kayla to see. But the glass had cracked and Daisy's wrinkles were like jagged edges revealing her pain.

"Why... " Kayla began, "why didn't you tell the police about this?"

Daisy crossed her arms forming an X over her chest and held herself tightly. "He asked a lot of questions, and after he left, Olaf pinched my arms again. He was so mad he wouldn't take me to the bathroom for the rest of the day. I ended up sitting in wet pants until Marta came. I didn't call the police. I didn't!" Her face was indignant, like a child who had been unjustly accused.

Kayla shrank back. "I called them, Daisy. I'm sorry. When I saw your face and thought you were saying 'Help me,' I didn't know what to do. Calling them seemed like the answer."

"Olaf will be home soon," Daisy said, "If he sees you here, he'll yell at me." Daisy clasped, then unclasped her hands.

Kayla slipped her the piece of paper she'd prepared. "Here's my phone number. Call if you need me."

"Marta helps me."

"Marta?" It was an unusual name but she'd seen or heard it before. "Is Marta your daughter?"

The dogs began barking. "Quick!" Daisy said.

Kayla rushed for the door, locking it behind her. *Did Rottweiler come back early?* The dogs lunged against the pen, but Kayla didn't see him. *Is he putting the snowmobile in the shed?*

Kayla hurried back through the calf-high snow, wishing there was a way to disguise her footprints. She quickly started her car. She just needed to back out of the driveway and she'd be safely gone. She put it in reverse and stepped on the accelerator. The front wheels spun, making the sickening whirring noise of a car stuck in deep snow. Panic rose to her chest. She had to get out of here. Now!

Rocking. That's what Rob did when he got stuck. She switched to drive, fed the car gas, then shifted to reverse. R-rrrrrr! Drive again, then reverse. Drive, reverse. It wasn't working. She searched for Rottweiler. *No sign of him yet. Maybe the dogs had barked at a passing squirrel.*

Her car clock said 6:40. He'd probably left the restaurant ten minutes ago. He'd be coming any second now. Kayla stepped on the gas again, only spinning deeper into the rut she'd made. A hot lump gathered in her throat. Then she remembered the shovel which her dad always insisted she keep in her trunk in case she had to dig her way out.

She grabbed her keys and opened the trunk. No shovel! She'd used it at the farm yesterday and never put it back. It was leaning against the rakes, but being able to picture its location perfectly wasn't helping her get out of this mess. She glanced toward Daisy's front window. Her face peered out at Kayla, and she looked sad, then scared, as a snowmobile's engine roared in the distance. Olaf Erickson was coming.

Kayla grabbed a knit cap she kept in the car and yanked it over her hair. Maybe Rottweiler wouldn't recognize her as the one who had trespassed earlier. Heart thumping, she stepped out of the car.

Rottweiler shut off the snowmobile motor then marched toward her, his red plaid jacket vivid against the white background. Kayla shuddered. Had it belonged to one of his dead friends?

"Hello," she said quickly. "I took a wrong turn and I'm afraid I'm lost."

"You sure are. This is private property."

"I'll be on my way as soon as I can get out of here." She looked at the tire rut.

Rottweiler gave a big sigh. "Looks like you'll have to call the wrecker."

"Could... could I use your phone?"

He looked toward the house. Daisy was still looking out. "I'll call for you," he said. "You wait in the car. Do you have a towing card?"

Mercifully, she found it quickly. He looked at it, reading her name, then handed it back to her. "Don't need your card to call."

Kayla stared after him as he lumbered toward the house. He had just wanted to read her name! He was as clever as Todd had said.

Daisy's face was visible in the picture window, but Kayla couldn't make out the expression. Was it fear or was she poker-faced, wanting to pretend ignorance? At Rottweiler's approach, the dogs yipped and lunged at the fence, tails wagging, probably hoping to be let out.

"Rip! Trucker! Quiet!" They stopped. Rottweiler stepped inside and the drapes immediately closed. Kayla's stomach lurched. If he wasn't guilty of abusing his wife, why was he so secretive? Why hadn't he invited Kayla into the house? Had he figured out that she knew he was hurting his wife?

When Rottweiler came back out he was smoking. His cold expression and the way he gripped the shovel made Kayla's heart thud against her ribs. He kept his distance, tossed his cigarette stub onto the snow and grumbled, "The wrecker's way out on the other side of town. I'm going to have to get you out of here. Hope you don't mind your floor mats being torn up."

Anything to escape, Kayla thought, but he didn't wait for an answer. He shoveled, then placed the car mats behind the front tires.

Mr. Erickson climbed in and started the car. Evidently, Kayla was to push. Kayla positioned herself by the front bumper. He shifted the car into reverse before Kayla expected and her attempt to push was late. Tires spun and whirred. "Are you pushing?" Mr. Erickson yelled. He didn't need to add "you idiot;" the silent message was there.

"Yes," Kayla said, gritting her teeth. The last thing she needed to do was get him angry, she told herself. "Try again."

Mr. Erickson again backed up. Kayla gave an extra hard push, and the wheels gripped, rolling out of the rut.

"All right!" Kayla cheered after he'd stepped around the car. She'd temporarily forgotten who she was talking to and why she'd come. As she threw the mats in the car, her cap slid back and strands of copper-colored hair fell out. Rottweiler stared at her.

"Uh," she stammered, "hang on while I get my purse."

"I don't want your money. Just leave us alone."

Now Kayla was sure he recognized her as the same redhead he'd sicced his dogs on. "All...all right, then. I'm sorry to have bothered you." She hurried behind the wheel, forcing herself not to tear out of the driveway. Every nerve in her body shouted *Hurry! Get away from this madman.* She scarcely breathed until she was back home.

○ ○ ○

As soon as she opened the door, she wanted to call Rob at the flower shop. But she knew he'd recognize how scared she was from her voice and leave work to come over. He might even make her promise not to go over there again. That promise couldn't be kept until she was sure Daisy was safe.

She waited until after nine o'clock. Then, even though her voice no longer revealed the terror she'd felt, Rob still said, "I hope you don't go over there again, but if you feel you have to, wait until I can come too."

"You work on Thursday and Saturday nights and those are the evenings I'm sure Rottweiler will be gone."

"Maybe I could get my schedule switched or maybe your aunt could go with you."

"I don't think Daisy would be as willing to talk if I brought another person. As soon as I find out if Marta is someone Daisy can turn to, I'll gladly stay away. Anyway, I'll call on Saturday night and once I know Marta's looking out for her, I won't worry anymore."

"At least calling is a lot safer than going over there." Rob sighed. "In fact, I wish you could work for that Nerad guy when you're guaranteed he won't show up. My hunches say there's something suspicious about a man who'd leave a high-paying job at a prestigious Ivy League university to teach here. I'm not sure who's scarier: Rottweiler or the mole."

○ ○ ○

The following afternoon Kayla remembered Rob's words when she entered the history office. *Dr. Nerad might be a bit different, but scary? Not really.*

"Good morning," a middle-aged receptionist said.

"Hi, I'm Kayla Montgomery. I'll be doing some work for Dr. Nerad and he said I should ask you for the key."

"Oh, yes, he mentioned a pretty girl would be coming by for it. I'll give you a time card and you can write down your hours. If you ask me, you ought to demand time and a half. No—double time!"

The secretary's words made more sense a few minutes later when Kayla opened the door. "I don't believe this," she said aloud. He couldn't have done a thing all week. She'd agreed to organize an office for what had to be the messiest professor in the universe! The room bulged with books. Some were shelved vertically, but if there was space above them, books were crammed in horizontally on top. Stacked piles stood from the floor, halfway to the ceiling. The large desk had so many papers and books scattered on top there wasn't a spot of wood showing. How could he work in here? She hadn't a clue where or how to start.

"Kayla?"

Kayla jumped. "Dr. Nerad!"

"Didn't mean to scare you. I saw your note saying you'd be here this morning and thought I'd ask if you needed anything. As you can see, I've pretty well cluttered my way out of my office."

"You sure have," Kayla said, sighing louder than she realized.

Dr. Nerad laughed.

Kayla felt herself blush, then admitted, "I have no idea how to tackle this."

"I must apologize for not warning you adequately." He winked, and said, "I was afraid you wouldn't take the job."

I probably wouldn't have, Kayla thought, looking around and discovering book piles under a table.

"I've been thinking about the solution and have decided to make the sacrifice. Every book over fifteen years old can be boxed up, then I'll haul them to my home and store them there. That should get rid of quite a few and the rest can be organized by author."

"All right," Kayla said, wondering about his wife's reaction when he came home with all those books. "This is a much bigger job than I'd thought, but I'll see what I can do." Now that there was a plan, she was suddenly anxious to get started. "Do you have some boxes?"

"The office has been saving some for me. I'll stop by occasionally in case you have questions." He leaned toward her and smiled. "Call if you need someone to dig you out." As he straightened back up, his hand brushed down her

39

arm. Kayla backed away. "Just a bit of organizing," he said, as if wanting to fill the silence.

Kayla let out a long breath after he left, then she laughed to herself. She was overreacting. The arm brushing might have been a fatherly gesture, or Dr. Nerad might be one of those people who hugged and touched a lot.

Kayla looked around and sighed. *The mole's burrow needed more than a bit of organizing. What it needed was a backhoe.*

She'd filled up four boxes by the time she looked at her watch. Yikes! She hadn't stopped for lunch and it was already time for her literature class. After that she'd have a few minutes to eat before psychology. Quickly sliding the boxes against the wall, she eyeballed the mess. Dr. Nerad could walk around if he pretended he was in a maze, but she didn't feel too badly because he couldn't possibly have worked in here before anyway. She'd come back as soon as she could and make more headway. One thing she didn't want was for him to come in and rearrange her stacks.

After locking the door, she strode to the office only to find it dark. *Ruby must have left for lunch, so what should I do with the key?* She quickly returned to Dr. Nerad's office, unlocked the door and wrote him a note. It said, "I worked until 11:45 and still have the key since the office was closed. I'll return Monday." She purposely didn't tell him Monday's time, as she didn't want him showing up again. After clearing away a pile of computer discs, a stack of papers and an open book, she set the note in the open space. Even then, she wasn't certain that he'd see it among all the clutter. Finally, she hurried to class.

○ ○ ○

When Rob picked her up that evening, Kayla avoided the discomfort of talking about Dr. Nerad and instead discussed Rottweiler. "He's scary," Kayla said as they traveled in the jeep down dark, country roads. "It's hard to believe there's someone so demented that he would hurt his helpless wife."

"You'd like to solve all the problems of the world, which is one of the things I love most about you." Rob covered her hand with his. "But, I don't think you understand it's not always possible."

"Maybe not, but it's worth a try."

"All right," Rob conceded, his lips curving up into half a smile. "I'm not going to lecture you. So, have you learned enough karate that you could take care of this Rottweiler character if you need to?"

"At my level, we're still advised to turn and run."

"Excellent advice," Rob said. His eyes sparked. "Why couldn't I have fallen in love with a girl whose idea of an excellent time is pizza and partying rather than risking her neck?"

Kayla smiled, but her thoughts turned to Liz Campbell, the girl Rob had dated last fall, who did fit his description. But she would not dwell on the past. Instead, Kayla asked, "When are you going to tell me where we're going?"

"We're almost there." Rob turned onto a logging road, and huge flakes of soft snow began falling as he parked.

Rob grabbed the backpack with their suits and towels and asked, "Are you going to be warm enough?"

"This goose down coat is super warm."

"Just what I had in mind." Rob had given it to her for Christmas, right before Luke, the other boy she'd been dating, had called to invite Kayla out to a fancy restaurant. Accepting that date had started an emotional roller coaster of dips and whirls.

Kayla took Rob's free arm as they walked down the snowy path. Dusk deepened into night and she said, "This is very romantic."

He bent down and kissed her. "I was hoping you'd feel that way. I thought about taking you to a restaurant or dancing, but that didn't seem special enough." Rob squeezed her hand. "It's wonderful to have you back in my life."

They were silent as they walked deeper into the pine forest. Kayla was surprised how much she could see once her eyes grew accustomed to the darkness.

"This ought to do it," Rob said, pulling out a small box.

"Do what? Why are we stopping? Are we on private property?"

"This land belongs to my boss, and he told me he's been hearing a barred owl, so I came out the other day and saw where it was roosting."

"You saw the owl?"

"Uh-huh, and there are a bunch of owl pellets under that big old pine. I'm hoping he, or she, is up there now."

"How will you know?"

Instead of answering, Rob took a wooden box out of his pocket and blew into it. "Who-cooks-for-you. Who-cooks-for-you-all."

They waited in silence. Kayla felt her heart hammering as she strained to hear and see. Since her eyes had adjusted to the darkness, it was amazing how much she could make out. Rob called once again. Soon after, the silhouette of an owl flew over them. The owl perched in a tree. Kayla held her breath for several minutes. Then, wonder of wonders, she heard a resounding *Whoo, whoo, whoo, whoo—whoo, whoo, whoo, whoo-ah.*

Kayla squeezed Rob's arm. "You try," he whispered excitedly, handing her the call.

Kayla took a deep breath and blew, "Who-cooks-for you. Who-cooks-for-you-all."

The owl answered *Whoo, whoo, whoo, whoo—woo, whoo, whoo, whoo-ah.*

"That is so terrific!" she whispered.

"I've tried this before," he said, "but never had an answer. You brought good luck. Oh, there she goes. Off to bring back dinner to the young."

"They have babies already?"

Rob nodded. "They nest early. The young are probably already fledged."

Suddenly, Kayla laughed.

"What's so funny?"

"You might be wanting a normal girlfriend, but how about me? My boyfriend's idea of impressing me is to walk around in the dark and hoot."

Rob laughed too. "But to be fair, you need to see the other part of my surprise. We're going to go back a different way."

"Where—"

"No questions," he teased, taking her arm. Once they were on their way, Rob said, "This would be a great activity to do with a group of kids at night. Maybe I'll get a chance sometime."

Kayla sighed, "You're lucky."

"I know I am," Rob said, squeezing her around the middle.

"I was referring to you knowing what you want to do with your life."

"I have a basic idea. A naturalist doesn't make a lot of money, but maybe I'll be able to pick up enough extra cash selling carvings or paintings."

Kayla nodded. "I need to make some decisions before I sign up for fall classes. Lately I've been thinking about being an elementary teacher."

"Elementary? I can see you doing that. You have a lot of patience, and you're great with little kids." They had come to a house and he swung her toward him so they could kiss. Afterward, he said, "You're an A+ kisser, too, but we won't tell your students that."

When they approached the house and he took a key out of his pocket to unlock the front door, she exclaimed, "What are you doing!"

"Bill's away for the weekend, and he said we could change inside and use his hot tub." He pointed to the covered hot tub on the deck.

"Okay," Kayla said, but the thought of him uncovering the tub and having to see the rising steam made her chest squeeze in panic. She'd never told Rob about her phobia. Besides, she was trying to get over it. Maybe this time she'd be able to handle it.

"You can use the bathroom to change—into your bikini," he added with a mischievous smile.

She dug into the backpack and pulled out her one-piece. "Sorry," she said, returning his smile and trying to sound carefree. "This is as skimpy as I get."

Rob changed in the bedroom and Kayla could hear him return to the deck. *He must be uncovering the hot tub.* After she adjusted her suit, Kayla looked out the window. Steam was rising from the hot tub. Images of that day when hot water had flowed into the bathtub threatened to surface, but she pushed them back down. She would control this.

When she walked out on the deck, Rob whistled. "Looking good there, lady. Let's hurry in and get warm."

I can do this. I can do this.

When she stared down at the steam, though, a wave of nausea overtook her. Sweat formed on her brow, and her legs turned to rubber. *Too much. Have to get away. Back inside. The couch. Make it to the couch.*

"Kayla? Are you all right?" Rob was right behind her.

"I thought I'd be able to do it, Rob, but I can't." She clasped her arms around her body. "I'm sorry. I should have told you before. I had a bad experience as a child." He arched his eyebrows. "When I was little I got scalded in the bathtub. Now whenever I'm surrounded by steam I—I sort of freak. I thought I could get past it, but..."

Rob sat beside her and held her close. "What happened?"

"Mom had left to answer the phone, and I wanted more bubbles so I got the box and dumped some in. Then I figured out I needed to add more water. I turned the wrong knob, though, and hot water poured out. I screamed and tried to get out, but the bubbles had made it so slippery I... I couldn't. Mom came running and lifted me out before I was badly burned, but the memory of that steam..."

"It's okay, honey." He squeezed her even closer.

She shivered violently and he said, "I'll take care of the hot tub. You change back into your warm clothes, then we'll go home." But as Rob flipped on a second outside light and returned to the deck, she sat watching through

46

the picture window, frozen in thought. *When Daisy's alone with Rottweiler, she must feel the same sense of helpless panic I just felt. Did he taunt her with a lit cigarette before he burned her? Did he grab her wrist to make her do something or to punish her?*

Rob returned, letting in a gust of wind. Kayla shuddered, the cold surrounding her like iron handcuffs around a helpless woman's wrist.

CHAPTER 4

Trapped

Saturday afternoon Kayla left work, then shopped. Ashley's birthday and the anniversary of the first time she met Rob were still almost a month away, but she wanted to make sure she wasn't rushed. Finding Ashley's birthday present was easy: cute bib overalls, a cuddly horse that looked like Sundance, and a beautifully illustrated version of *Mother Goose*. Rob's was more difficult. For one thing, it wasn't exactly a one year anniversary for them. With all their ups and downs, six months was closer to the truth. Still, she wanted to find something that represented how they had grown as a couple. After seeing a sculpture of a hen and tom turkey at a gift shop, she told the owner she might be back.

Kayla was still thinking about the sculpture when she pulled into the driveway and saw her mother hurrying out the front door carrying a suitcase. *What on earth?* Mom hefted it into the open trunk then hurried toward Kayla.

"Hi, honey," she said in a delicate voice that meant she was worried. "We've been trying to find you."

"I was shopping," Kayla said, her heart hammering. "What's wrong?"

Mom gave her a hug. "It's Grandpa," she said, tears welling in her eyes. "He's had a heart attack and has slipped into a coma."

Grandpa! Mom was saying something about tickets for a five o'clock flight to Birmingham, but Kayla heard little past those dreaded words *heart attack*. "Aunt Maggie wondered if you'd take care of her place. She wants to come, too."

"What about Ashley?"

"She'll bring her along, although we may have to ask some friends to babysit."

"I wish I could come, too," Kayla said.

"I know, but you've got school and frankly we don't know what else to do. There isn't time to explain to someone else how to care for the horses—"

Kayla realized they must be afraid he'd die at any moment. Why the big hurry, otherwise?

Mom said, "If only Uncle Jim hadn't left for Russia."

Kayla said, "Don't worry, Mom. Let's hope Grandpa will get better, and I can see him when he comes for a visit. Will there be someplace I can call to find out what's happening?"

"Yes, of course. We'll call and give you a number. Oh, I called the Coopers, the people Joey's staying with, to let them know he may have problems in school. He's used to having me there and this may throw him for a loop. I told them if they want, I can call Joey at home. They'll call you here if they want me to do that."

Even in this much of a hurry, Mom worries about Joey? Kayla could hardly believe it.

Mom sighed. "We'd better leave now."

"When will I hear from you?"

"Tonight, but it'll be late." Mom gave her one more lingering glance. "I hate to leave you—"

Two suitcases in hand, Dad whisked out of the door. "Are you okay with staying here, sweetie?" Kayla nodded. "Sorry to have to rush off like this, but we're trying to make the plane. Remember to lock the doors and use good judgment."

"I will, Dad."

He looked at his watch. "Come on, Karen, we have to go." Dad gave Kayla a kiss. "Take care of yourself."

"Tell Grandma I'll be thinking about everyone," Kayla said, "and wishing I could be there." With a last wave, they were gone.

Kayla looked around in amazement. How quickly things could change! As she cleaned up the lunch dishes left in the kitchen, she thought about Grandpa. It had been over three years since they'd traveled to Alabama to see him and Grandma. She had just been telling Rob about the night she, Ned, and Grandpa had taken a moonlit walk in the dunes. She and Ned had been trying to catch an especially large white ghost crab before it escaped into a hole when, suddenly, Ned had screamed. Then she felt the burning stings, too. Fire ants! She had grabbed Ned's hand, but Grandpa was quicker. He'd carried him far away from the mound, then helped them both brush off the biting ants. She sighed. It was hard to imagine Grandpa unable to even raise his arm now. *Wake up, Grandpa,* Kayla prayed. *Please wake up.*

Kayla had almost finished cleaning up when the phone rang. She picked it up. "Kayla," a feeble voice said, "I need you. Come quick." Click.

"Daisy? Is that you?" But the line was dead. She was sure that had been Daisy's voice, but why had she hung up so abruptly? Had Rottweiler discovered her placing the call? Had he hurt her again?

Fingers fumbling, she paged through the phone book. No Olaf Erickson. She called the operator only to find his number was unlisted.

Did she dare go over there? Should she call the police first? Officer Bork's words echoed in her head. *If you do have some hard and fast evidence of abuse, call me back.* She didn't have any evidence yet, but she might shortly.

It was just after four and Olaf would be with his trapping buddies for almost another two and a half hours. How should she go to Daisy's house? If she drove, she'd take a chance at getting stuck again and she'd leave tracks for Rottweiler to question. She'd better go on horseback.

First, she'd let Rob know her plans. He didn't answer his phone though and she had to leave a message. Finally, she defrosted a hunk of meat in the microwave. It was time to make friends with those dogs.

Kayla had Taffy, the caramel and cream paint, saddled and ready to go by four-thirty. Taffy moved right along, but it was still 5:15 before they got to the house. As soon as they rounded the bend, the dogs started barking. Kayla's stomach muscles tightened. She needed to do this one last time, she told herself, hoping to keep panic from rising in her throat. After tonight she could turn the responsibility over to Marta or... to the police.

Hearing the ferocious barking made Taffy snort. "It's all right," Kayla said. "They're in a pen and can't get you. I'll tie you back here, though, so you're not so close to them." Kayla tied the mare to a tree, then pulled the bloody package out of the saddlebag. She hiked the rest of the way in, hoping another snowfall would cover her tracks. She approached the barking dogs.

They jumped and lunged at the mesh fence, jogging Kayla's memory of their attack. Those sharp, yellowish-white teeth had slashed Sundance. Kayla unwrapped the meat and stepped closer. The dogs followed her to the spot, still lunging. She tossed a piece of round steak over the fence and they fought one another for it. Kayla threw them a second piece and headed to the house. She tossed the blood-stained wrapper into an outdoor trash can and checked for the snowmobile. It was gone, but an older model van was parked in its place.

The doorbell was answered almost immediately. When the door opened, Kayla stepped back in surprise. A huge buxom woman with cropped hair said, "Yes?" She was round-faced and big-boned like Rottweiler. She wiped her huge hands on her oversized t-shirt while Kayla struggled for words.

"Uh…. I'm Kayla Montgomery," she finally managed to say. "I met Daisy last week and just wanted to stop by and see how she was doing."

"You met her last week? How?"

The words came out rudely, but Kayla thought the woman was more curious than anything. "I was trail riding, and she was watching from the window."

The whir of Daisy's wheelchair sounded closer. "Is that the horse girl?" she asked.

"Yes," the large woman said.

"Let her in."

The door opened wider and Kayla stepped inside. "Sorry about this," the younger woman said with a lilt in her voice. "You caught me off guard. Dad doesn't usually like strangers coming 'round."

"Oh," Kayla said, both anxious and relieved. "You're Daisy's daughter?"

"Yes, I'm Marta."

Kayla reached out and shook Marta's man-sized hand. "Glad to meet you."

"Have a seat." While Kayla sat in a wooden rocker, she wondered if Marta would be more sympathetic towards her mom or her dad. *Had Daisy told her about her dad pinching her and not taking her to the bathroom?* "Excuse me a moment," Marta said, "while I turn off the stove."

The smell of meat cooking mingled with the stale smell of cigarettes in the airless room. After Marta left, Kayla asked, "How are you doing, Daisy?"

"Not so good." She shook her head, drawing attention to her matted curls in need of brushing. "I never get out of this place."

"Did you call me on the phone?" Kayla asked.

Just then Marta returned and sat on the couch. Daisy asked, "Did you bring your horse?" giving Kayla the feeling she didn't want Marta to know about the phone call.

"Actually I brought my aunt's horse this time." Kayla would have liked to add that her horse had gotten a leg slashed from her husband's dogs.

Daisy said, "I was a champion rider. I took first place in jumping at the state fair."

"Yes, I know." Kayla didn't mind that Daisy repeated herself. She was obviously proud.

"I sure would love to ride a horse again." Daisy wiggled in her chair.

Kayla looked at Daisy thoughtfully. She wished she knew how disabled Daisy really was. Would she be able to wrap her legs around, hang onto the reins, kick if she wanted to trot? Could she walk at all?

"Would you take me?" Daisy's eyes moistened and she looked at Kayla.

Kayla looked at Marta and stumbled, "I... I'm not sure."

Marta answered, "I could lift her up there. She'd be fine if you lead the horse."

Kayla glanced at her watch. Only half an hour before Rottweiler would return. As if reading her mind, Marta said, "We should probably wait until another time when Dad's gone again. He's funny about outsiders."

Kayla breathed a sigh of relief. She didn't want to risk running into him again. "How about Thursday night?"

"That'd be fine," Marta said. "I have an appointment with my attorney earlier, but I should be done before four. Could you come then?"

Kayla nodded.

"Marta likes to ride, too," Daisy hinted.

"Yes, I do," the woman said. She must have been in her mid-fifties with clear skin and one obvious black moustache hair. *Why in the world didn't she pluck it out?* "I lost my horse when that... when my ex-husband..." Marta sighed. "I better not get started on that. Oh, I smell the sauce."

After she left for the kitchen, Kayla said, "I'm sorry to come at supper time. I just wanted to check on you. Daisy, are you all right? Can you talk to Marta if you need something?"

"Marta? Pftt. She's hardly around. When she decides to take off, she just gets in her car and goes. Leaves me here—with him. She always was selfish. Her and her hippy friends. Going off camping, backpacking, looking at old rock drawings."

"Pictographs, Mom," Marta said, returning in time to hear the last sentence. "Actually, some were petroglyphs or carvings."

"Painted or carved," Daisy grumbled, "they're still gibberish."

Kayla leaned forward at the edge of the rocker. "My Native American culture professor has talked about rock art. Where did you go to see them?"

"I went with a group to Arizona. We were backpacking and camping, but there are impressive pictographs just forty miles from here."

"Really?"

"Yes. I'd love to see them again. The only trouble is it's quite a ways in from the road, and I've torn the ligaments in my left foot so I'm not keen on going for a long hike. I know some people who have gone back on horses." She glanced at Kayla.

Marta was hinting and Kayla was tempted. A day trip with Marta would be a perfect opportunity to talk to her about her mother. "Maybe you and I could go," Kayla said. "I could use my aunt's pickup and trailer. Sundance is nearly well enough to go, and you could ride Taffy."

"Hey! That sounds great. Let's talk about it Thursday when we give Mom a ride." Marta smiled at her mother and she smiled back.

Kayla glanced at her watch. Rottweiler would be roaring up soon, and she needed to tend the horses. "I have to go," she said squatting down by Daisy's chair so they were eye to eye, "but I'll see you Thursday."

"See you later, alligator," Daisy said, smiling.

As Kayla rode Taffy back in the fading light, she realized instead of ending the relationship, she'd made a commitment for a trail riding adventure on Thursday and a day trip with Marta. *So much for avoiding getting involved.*

Kayla called Rob as soon as she returned to assure him she'd survived the trip to Daisy's and to tell him about Marta. She kept the conversation short, though, hoping Mom would call with news about Grandpa. When the phone rang at 11:30 and Mom's quivering voice said there wasn't any change, Kayla felt a soft ache in her throat. Grandpa just had to get better.

In the morning she cared for the horses, all the while thinking about Grandpa and Daisy. They were both trapped: Grandpa's mind not able to resurface, Daisy's body not strong enough to fight off her husband or leave.

It was while she was cleaning out Sundance's wounds that she formed other questions for Marta. *Had she considered getting her dad into therapy or counseling? Did he possibly have a mental illness that caused him to hurt his wife? Was there anything that could be done?*

On Monday morning her mother called. Grandpa was still in a coma. Aunt Maggie sounded as drained as Mom. "We'd like to stay the week," she said. "Is that all right?"

"Of course," Kayla said. "Stay as long as you need."

Aunt Maggie asked, "Is everything all right? With the Erickson's? I hope you're not taking any foolish chances."

Kayla wasn't about to add to Aunt Maggie's worries so she simply said, "Everything's okay. I'll fill you in when you come back. Give Grandpa a kiss for me."

"Will do, honey. Take care now."

Helpless to assist her family, Kayla funneled her energy into caring for the horses, working at the museum, and attending classes. She forced herself to concentrate and took careful notes during Dr. Nerad's lecture. At the end of class, he stopped her. "I see you made quite a bit of progress in my office."

"Yes. I'm planning on coming back tomorrow."

"Oh, what time?"

She hesitated only a fraction of a second. It was safe to say since she'd be coming over the supper hour. "I thought I'd come around five-thirty." She tried out what she hoped was a charming grin. "In between study sessions."

He smiled back. "Far be it from me to impede that."

○ ○ ○

As Kayla arrived the next afternoon, a group of secretaries was leaving. The halls became deserted and eerily quiet. Her first instinct was to follow the women out. How had she gotten herself into this? She took a deep breath and told herself she'd be able to get a lot done with no one around. As soon as she unlocked the door, she switched on the radio she'd uncovered the last time and found a peppy station. She'd filled six boxes and the place was starting to look like an office when a shadow filled the doorway. "Oh!" she gasped. "Dr. Nerad! You startled me."

She hurried to turn off the radio.

"Sorry," he said. "I would have warned you, but the radio was on so loud." He was smiling.

"I'm making progress," she said.

"Yes, I'll say you are. In fact, I can see the top of my desk. I'll clear these boxes out tomorrow."

"Is it all right if I continue a few more minutes?"

"Go right ahead."

Kayla bent over a stack of books, but he was watching her and it made her uneasy. She read a framed certificate while wiping it off. *The Chancellor's Award for Excellence in Teaching.* He'd gotten that his first semester here! "You ought to hang this up," Kayla said.

He reached for it. "Yes, I'm quite proud of this award. After you're done, I'll find a spot for it."

"I thought I'd just sort through this pile," Kayla said. "Then I should be able to finish on Friday, unless I have to meet with my advisor." Kayla sighed.

"Problems with career choices?"

Kayla frowned. "It's so hard to narrow it down."

Dr. Nerad nodded. "It's tough, all right. It's helpful to talk to people in the fields you're interested in."

"Yes, I'll remember that." The wall clock buzzed loudly and Kayla said, "Well, I better get back to work." She shifted her attention to the pile of books.

Dr. Nerad sat at his desk, now only partially cluttered. "I've got a few papers to read if you don't mind."

Kayla couldn't very well say she'd prefer he left. Trying not to be distracted, she continued to sort through the pile. Dr. Nerad shuffled papers. Finally, brushing her hands together and stepping back, she said, "Enough for tonight. I'll head home now."

Dr. Nerad said, "It's looking great. Let's go out for a cup of coffee to celebrate."

"Now?"

"It's just seven-thirty."

A professor, one who had received a prestigious award, published several books, and taught at Cornell, wanted to spend time with her! Still, it felt kind of creepy. Not that the guy would be coming on to her. After all, he was at least twenty years older and married. Dr. Nerad waited.

"Do you like lattés?" he finally asked.

"I've never had one."

"Come on, then. I've got a treat for you. It'll be a good opportunity for us to talk about career choices, too. Maybe I can help steer you to the right courses to take next semester."

He led the way. Kayla followed him out the door. She would like to hear his opinion on career options and if she felt anxious, she'd just suddenly remember needing to get up early the next morning and she'd ask him to take her back.

Professor Nerad drove a Subaru. It looked fairly new, but had a dent in the front bumper. "Did you or your wife have an accident?" Kayla asked, letting him know she knew he was married.

"Clarisse did. She has a perception problem, among other health concerns, and this latest claim caused the insurance company to drop us."

Other health concerns? Kayla wasn't sure how to respond.

They parked at a Holiday Inn. Kayla asked, "Does Holiday Inn have a coffee bar?"

"No, but they do offer several different types on their menu."

As the hostess brought them to the table, Dr. Nerad slipped Kayla's black wool blazer from her shoulders. "That's okay," she said, reaching for it, but he was already

61

heading for the coat room. Her black-lace top wasn't exactly appropriate without the blazer, but she wasn't going to chase him down and make a big deal out of it.

After Dr. Nerad returned, he said, "They have decaf turtles, too, if you don't want caffeine this late at night." His tone was fatherly and Kayla relaxed.

"I'd like to try the latté," she said. "Explore new horizons, I always say." Kayla felt awkward, not sure whether to play the role of employee, student, or acquaintance. She doubted she'd be able to impress Dr. Nerad with travel stories or entertain him with her daily life, so she better settle for the student slot. She was best at asking questions.

When the waitress appeared, Dr. Nerad read her name tag. "Good evening, Edith. My companion and I would both like a latté. Doesn't she look charming this evening?"

Edith glanced at Kayla, stared a second at her top, then nodded. After she left, Dr. Nerad looked at her. "You're very pretty," he said suddenly.

Kayla shifted. This was feeling like a mistake. He was studying her reaction. "Thank you," she said quickly.

"You remind me of my wife before she stopped taking care of herself. Clarisse was quite attractive, but for years now, she's let herself go. She's gained thirty pounds and doesn't fix herself up."

Kayla wished she could think of a graceful way to leave.

"I try to support her emotionally, but she seems so far away. It's nice to come here with you and relax. No," he said contemplating, "this is more than relaxing. I'm really enjoying myself."

Mercifully, the waitress arrived with the coffee. Kayla quickly picked it up and took a sip. "M-mmm" she said. "Lattés are good."

"I'm glad you're enjoying exploring new horizons," he teased. Her expression seemed to take on a different meaning when he said it. "Foreign foods, travel and new experiences help broaden a person, and if my guess is right, you're someone who wants to live life to the fullest."

Maybe he'd invited her out to share some of his experiences, tell the stories of his life. She felt much more comfortable with that thought. But he didn't continue. Instead he asked, "So, have you chosen your major yet?"

"I'm thinking about education. I'd like to go into counseling or maybe teach."

Dr. Nerad nodded. "Both challenging fields." His voice had slipped into the professor mode, rising in pitch at the end of every sentence. "Would you be an elementary teacher?"

"Probably. I might specialize in emotionally disturbed children. My mother is an aide for the Special Education teacher at school, so I know a bit of what it would be like."

Dr. Nerad nodded. "And I imagine you're wanting a MRS degree, too?"

It took Kayla a minute to understand what he was saying, then she blushed. "No, not for quite a while."

"Does that mean you've ruled out marriage?"

Now Kayla was back to feeling tense. "No, I'd like to get married and have kids one day."

"I hope you won't mind a bit of advice. Make sure your chosen mate has the same educational background you have. That's very important." His voice dropped. "My wife dropped out of college. It's not that she's not intelligent, it's more that we don't have the same zest for improving ourselves. Now you strike me as being quite intelligent."

Kayla's face burned. She needed to get on more comfortable ground. "I have a friend," she began, "a white girl who's dating a Native American. She's worried about the differences in their two cultures."

"She should be. Take the example of a Protestant marrying a Catholic and multiply it by ten. It won't be an easy route, for either one of them." Dr. Nerad squinted his eyes until they were nearly invisible. "She has to make sure she's in love with the person, not fascinated with the culture. Do you think she's enjoying the attention she gets from being in an interracial relationship?"

Kayla visualized Josie's wild hair, outlandish clothes, and right ear pierced in seven places. "She enjoys drawing attention, so she might be."

"So, tell me," he continued, "are you in a relationship?"

"Yes. My boyfriend's name is Rob. He goes to Nicolet, too."

Dr. Nerad nodded.

Kayla abruptly asked, "Have you done any traveling?"

Dr. Nerad blinked in surprise. Her transition to another topic hadn't been very smooth. Kayla took another long drink, hoping to finish and leave.

"Yes," he answered, "but not lately. I was in the Navy and did my traveling then. The worst four years of my life." He shook his head. "No privacy, no normal activities.... So, where would you like to travel?"

"Australia would be high on my list and so would France. I'm minoring in French."

"Le gay Paris," Dr. Nerad said. "The city of romance. I can understand that, but why Australia?"

"I met a man from Australia last summer. His family raises sheep in the outback. The way he described Ayers Rock and the countryside made me want to see it someday."

"This young man," Dr. Nerad asked, "were you attracted to him?"

Kayla's face warmed.

"I see you were. I didn't think girls blushed anymore. I'm glad to see they do. Hmm, you the wife of an Australian sheep herder," he mused. "I can't picture it. You would need more stimulus. You'd dry up in that atmosphere. Your lovely skin would turn to leather and after the third baby you'd lose that great figure."

Kayla took the last sip and set the cup down noisily. He didn't take the hint.

"So, tell me," Dr. Nerad asked in a husky voice. "What do you think of me?"

Kayla blinked, her face flaming hot. "I... I think you're a great professor—"

"I don't mean as a professor." *As a man then?* Kayla visualized an iceberg, 10% on top of the surface and 90% below. Her top 10% was flattered that a highly acclaimed professor was interested in her, but the rest of her shuddered with revulsion. *This was creepy and wrong.* He was still staring at her. Kayla stood. "I... I think I'd better get back." He raised his eyebrows, but silently retrieved her blazer. He held it while she slipped her arms in the sleeves. Kayla's flesh recoiled at his touch. He lingered, positioning the jacket on her back. She felt an urge to run. Every nerve in her body was on alert. As he paid the bill, the absurdity of his question pulsed in her head. *Did he want to know if I found him handsome? Was he coming on to me?*

The professor kept the conversation neutral on the trip back home. Kayla's responses were brief. Only when she was safely in her car on campus did she breathe easily again. If her instincts were right, she'd rather face Rottweiler or the vicious dogs than be alone with creepy Nerad again.

CHAPTER 5

Burning Questions

Two days later, Thursday, Grandpa's condition still hadn't changed. "Aunt Maggie and I feel we should stay a bit longer," Mom said over the phone. "I hate being away from work and from you, but I'm needed here. Grandma isn't handling this well. She can't stay alone and we're looking into different possibilities. How are things going there?"

"Fine," Kayla said with little hesitation. "In fact, Sundance's leg has healed so well I'm riding her later." Kayla prayed Mom wouldn't ask where.

"That's great. All right, honey. You take care of yourself. I'll call tomorrow."

An hour later, Kayla had Sundance saddled. The mare was eager to go, and it was only when they came to the ridge where they'd been attacked that Sundance's ears flattened. She looked around as if expecting to see the dogs come ripping toward her. As it was, when they approached the house and Sundance heard their barking, the horse threw back her head.

"It's okay, girl. They're in the pen and they aren't going to hurt you." Kayla tied Sundance to a tree, wishing she could get her closer so Marta wouldn't have to carry Daisy so far. But Kayla didn't want to upset Sundance.

Kayla had brought two chunks of hamburger and when she fed the dogs, their growls changed into chomps and slurps.

Marta let her inside the house. "Aw," Marta exclaimed. "I just got out of the steam room." She patted her red face. "After meeting with my lawyer, I needed a chance to unwind. It's great for achy muscles, but that thermostat must be on the fritz again. It was hotter than blazes."

Kayla shuddered. "Steam rooms aren't for me. I got scalded in a bathtub when I was little. I still get panicky when I'm near anything with steam."

"Mom used to love the steam room," Marta said, handing Daisy her hat and gloves. "In fact, Dad had it added for her as a birthday present shortly after they moved in. It used to be a storage closet for things the old owners didn't want their kids getting into." She pointed to the deadbolt. Daisy was busy getting ready and didn't appear to be listening. "It's harder to get Mom in and out of it now since she broke her hip."

"Oh," Kayla said in a low voice. She'd wondered why Daisy was in a wheelchair. "When did that happen?"

"Over a year ago. It didn't heal properly." Marta shook her head. "It's too bad because Mom used to be very active."

Daisy grinned and announced, "The horse woman is all set!"

"Sundance is ready, too," Kayla said.

68

"I used to have a Saddlebred," Daisy said as Marta lifted her effortlessly, and Kayla held the front door open. "He was all black and his name was... What was his name, Marta?"

"We called him TNT."

Daisy giggled. "That's right. He unloaded both your father and me before we cured him." Daisy's expression was dreamy. "Olaf bought him for me." Kayla frowned. *Had Olaf truly loved Daisy once? What happened to change him?*

The dogs gave a few half-hearted barks, but their looks were more expectant than hostile. As Marta's boots crunched down the snowy slope, Daisy said, "Look at this nice white carpet." She giggled. "A little cold to roll around on, though." Suddenly Daisy squealed, "I can see her! There's—" She turned to Kayla for help.

"Sundance," Kayla finished.

"She's beautiful."

Barely out of breath, Marta lifted her mother into Sundance's saddle. Kayla was amazed at Marta's strength and wondered if she lifted weights or worked out.

Kayla had attached a lead rope to Sundance but gave Daisy reminders of how to steer and stop so she could feel she was in control. Daisy wore a big grin as they set out. She turned back to Marta and waved. "Don't hold supper for me," she teased.

"All right, Ma. Have fun."

"I was a champion rider," Daisy said as Sundance walked along and Kayla tried to keep up in the snow. She hadn't thought of how hard it would be for her to walk, but Daisy's bright smile made the effort worthwhile. The woman playfully moved the reins. Kayla tried to lead Sundance the way Daisy turned the reins until Daisy flip-flopped them quickly then watched for Kayla's reaction. Kayla met her teasing eyes and laughed. "Are you having fun with me?"

"I'm having fun," Daisy agreed.

Kayla grinned in satisfaction. At least she'd been able to do that much.

Daisy brought up the state fair again, as if unaware she'd already told Kayla about it. "I took first place, you know. The third rail was a solid wall, and I knew Micky would balk at it, so I kicked her hard and whispered, 'We can do this.' Sailed up and over, we did. Could have jumped it if it had been five feet high." Daisy threw back her shoulders.

Kayla recalled her own memory of jumping the gorgeous American Saddlebred, Black Magic, when she'd been a counselor at the dude ranch. He was powerful enough to jump two hay bales and possibly even three. Yes, Kayla also loved the feeling of being lifted high above the ground and sailing effortlessly through the air.

"Ah," Daisy continued, "jumping always made me so happy." *Daisy added, "I've never felt quite that happy since." She stared at something in the distance and her shoulders slumped. Kayla was about to ask her if* something was wrong when Daisy blurted out, "I went to a country school." The sudden change in mood and subject was startling, but Kayla was getting used to Daisy's personality shifts. "I had a really mean teacher for the fourth and fifth grades. Mrs. Brewster hid a ruler up her left sleeve, and if we so much as whispered, she'd haul it out and crack the back of our hands."

"That's awful—" Kayla began, but Daisy interrupted.

"She took us to the dark furnace room if we talked back or misbehaved. Would whip us until we cried. Once I was taken there for poking Billy Fischer in the back with a pencil. He'd been sliding around on his wool pants giving me shocks all morning, but when I tried to tell old lady Brewster that, she wouldn't listen. She grabbed me so tightly by the arms I had bruises for weeks. That day I told myself I wouldn't cry out. She beat me until she drew blood. I came home and when my parents saw me, she was fired." Daisy nodded her head in satisfaction. "We took care of her."

If only she had that same gumption when it came to standing up to her husband! Kayla thought.

They had rounded the corner and were approaching the steep hill where Rip and Trucker had attacked Sundance. "We better turn back around here," Kayla said. "It gets pretty steep."

Daisy was tiring, and Kayla knew if she wanted to ask her questions, she had to start now. "Daisy," she began, "you mentioned a few minutes ago that you haven't felt happy for a while. Can you tell me what's wrong? Maybe I can help." When she didn't answer, Kayla prodded, "Is Olaf treating you all right?"

"Olaf took me to a dance for our first date," Daisy began. Had she misheard Kayla or couldn't she deal with the question? "His older brother and my brother were friends." She looked off toward the house. "My, how handsome he looked that night: black, wavy hair, strong body, and the greenest eyes that a gal could imagine."

Kayla agreed that Rottweiler could be handsome if he would smile or look less gruff. Kayla gave Sundance a pat. "Mr. Erickson is a good husband, isn't he?" Kayla held her breath.

Daisy raised her sleeve and rubbed her arm. "Daisy!" Kayla pulled back on the reins. "What happened?" An ugly red burn, the size of a dime, scarred her arm.

"Mean," Daisy said. "Olaf and Marta are both mean."

Marta too? Was it possible? Were they both abusing her? A roar went up through Kayla's mind and she wanted to scream, *How dare they do this to you! Why do you let them? Your own husband! Your own daughter!*

Daisy sang out, "I took the championship at the Madison hunter jumper show when I was in high school." A cold shiver raced up and down Kayla's spine. Daisy was back in her dream world. *Was Daisy's bizarre behavior an attempt to block out painful memories,* or—and this thought made Kayla's heart race even faster—*was Daisy being drugged? If Marta or Olaf wanted a confused victim, drugs would be a way to do it. But why would they want her this way?* Kayla wished she didn't have such an active imagination.

Daisy rubbed her arm again. "Cigarette," she said, then whined, "are we almost home?"

Cigarette. Had someone burned her with a cigarette? "Yes, Daisy, we're almost home," Kayla said chewing on her bottom lip. How was she going to handle this?

After tying up Sundance, Kayla looked at her watch. It was already six o'clock. Rottweiler would be leaving the restaurant in half an hour. She might have just enough time to ask Marta about Daisy's burn mark."

Marta must have heard the dogs barking because she was waiting at the edge of the woods. The big woman whisked her mother off the horse and carried her toward the house, calling over her shoulder, "Come inside when you're finished."

After Kayla tied Sundance, she followed. Marta, who'd put her mother back in the wheelchair asked, "Are we still on for the trip to Painted Falls?"

"Y-yes, but I need to talk to you. Alone," she whispered.

Marta motioned for her to follow her into the kitchen. She pulled out a pack of cigarettes and lit one up. "What's up?"

"Your mother's burn," Kayla began.

Marta quickly set her cigarette in an ashtray. "Oh, isn't it awful? She heard the oven timer while I was in the bathroom and took it upon herself to try to get a casserole out of the oven. Her in a wheelchair!" Red blotches appeared on Marta's neck.

"Oh," Kayla said, biting her bottom lip. *The burn mark's shaped exactly like the end of a cigarette,* she thought. *And Daisy had mumbled "cigarette" while she'd rubbed it. Is Marta lying?*

"So," Marta said, "when would you like to go see the pictographs?"

It took a moment for Kayla to shift focus. Maybe if she spent the day with Marta she'd have a better clue as to what was going on. "Would this Saturday work?"

"Let me check my purse calendar." Marta headed to a back bedroom leaving Kayla in the kitchen. Kayla checked her watch. Six-thirty. *Olaf is on his way back.*

Marta returned and said, "Saturday will be great? Should I meet you at the Norton's farm and help load the horses?"

"Okay," Kayla said heading for the door. "Around ten?"

"Fine."

She was about to leave when she realized this would be a perfect opportunity to get Marta's phone number in case she needed to call. Maybe she should get Daisy's too. "Could I have your number in case something comes up?"

"I don't have a phone—" Marta began, but stopped when she heard the unmistakable roar of the snowmobile.

Kayla caught Daisy's expression. The old woman's look of dread probably mirrored her own.

"Good-bye," Kayla said hastily, hand on the knob. But as she opened it, the engine's roar came to an abrupt stop and Rottweiler yelled, "Hold it!"

Kayla froze in the open doorway as he lumbered toward her. Absurd as it was, all Kayla could think about was that he'd left early.

"What the hell is going on here?" His face was hard, eyes only narrow slits.

When Marta didn't say anything, Kayla found her courage and said, "I took your wife for a horseback ride. That's all."

Marta chimed in, "That's right, Mom had a great time."

Olaf looked from Marta to Kayla to Daisy. Daisy had shrunk back in her wheelchair. "I told her I didn't want to go, Olaf," she said desperately. "I'm going to my room now."

As the whir of the wheelchair faded away, the heavy muscles of Rottweiler's face tightened and drew into ugly knots. His eyes glazed furiously at Kayla. "This is the second time you've come here interfering." Rottweiler stepped forward until his face was inches from hers and she could smell his cigarette breath. His words were soft, dangerously soft. "Leave and don't you ever come back, or you'll be facing a lawsuit so high you'll never see daylight."

"Now, Daddy," Marta said, coming over to him. "There's nothing to be upset about."

Kayla's only thought was of escape. "Good-bye," she said to Marta. Mercifully, she had her hand on the knob, then she was out the door. Safe. After passing the dogs, she looked back. Rottweiler was talking to Marta in a far corner, away from Daisy. *So, they might very well be in this together. What are they talking about? Would he take his anger out on Daisy?* With more questions than answers, Kayla rejoined Sundance and mounted.

On the way home, Kayla tried to figure out what had happened. *Why hadn't Marta spoken up right away and defended my presence? Was she afraid of her father? Did Daisy really burn herself?* Kayla hoped that on Saturday, Marta would say something that would help explain.

○ ○ ○

The next morning the same questions and a few more buzzed in Kayla's head while she finished chores and headed to Nicolet. She'd planned on finishing Dr. Nerad's library from 10:30-12:00 while he had a class so she wouldn't have to worry about facing him. Having to sit through history later in the afternoon would be uncomfortable enough. How would she be able to look at him, remembering that he'd asked her what she thought of him. *Was that just an innocent question or had he meant more by it?*

The work went well and at 11:45, Kayla stood back. She'd done it. Every book was in place, titles displayed, and arranged by author. And, she realized glancing at her watch, she'd finished in time. His class would just be getting over. She debated about leaving a note, but in the end simply locked the door and headed to the history office. Ruby was already at lunch. *What to do with the key? Better keep it for now.*

That afternoon, Kayla had trouble focusing on Nerad's Civil War lecture. As the students filed out he said, "Oh, Miss Montgomery. May I see you?"

Kayla hung back and after everyone had left he said, "You're remarkable, magical actually. I'm recommending you for a purple heart."

"So, you like how it turned out?"

"I'm more than satisfied. How about celebrating with me tonight? It's the end of the week and my office is in tiptop shape." He smiled sheepishly. "It will probably never look this good again. What do you say? We could go back to the Holiday Inn. They have a cajun cook and he makes the best jambalaya north of Louisiana."

"I have class."

"Only until 7:30."

How did he know that? Kayla's stomach turned queasy. "I'm sorry Dr. Nerad, but I can't."

"How else are you going to get your check?" he teased, lifting his eyebrows suggestively.

"I really need to get home tonight. I have to read the three chapters you assigned." She attempted a wry smile.

"They aren't due until Monday," he countered.

"Still, I want to get a start on them. History isn't my strong suit and with next week's midterm...."

"You won't need to worry about the midterm," he said, his voice low, eyelids slightly drooped.

The hairs on the back of Kayla's neck rose. All she wanted was to get out of there. "I need to go," she croaked abruptly and pushed past him out the door.

Outside in the brisk air she shook her head. He couldn't have possibly meant that if she went out with him tonight, he'd give her a good grade on the midterm. No way would he dare do anything like that. Yet his voice and manner were creepy, and the back of her neck felt like little bugs were crawling on it.

Her friend Josie was waiting. Josie's hair was just past her ears, and styled as if she were preparing to shoot an MTV video. She wore jewelry of her own design and had tucked a purple crocus behind one ear. "Finally," Josie said. "You've been hard to track down."

"Me? You're the one who's never home."

Josie shrugged. "Well, how have you been?"

"How much time do you have?"

"Next class starts in five minutes."

Where to begin? Do I say I'm worried that Daisy is being abused or that Nerad may have just made a sexual advance and I'm afraid to talk to Rob about it? In the end all Kayla said was, "It's complicated. Maybe it should wait."

"All right. I know—since Wednesday's your birthday, let's have one of our famous all-night talk sessions." Josie grinned. "I've got a few stories of my own to share."

"Wednesday then."

Saturday morning dawned cool but bright. Kayla told Rob on the phone, "I need to find out more about Marta. It's hard to believe she'd be mean to her own mother. Daisy was telling the truth about being afraid of her, though. I could see the fear in her eyes."

"Maybe it isn't such a great idea to be alone with Marta."

"Oh, she's not going to hurt me. She'd have no reason."

Rob said, "Still, be careful. I'd like to keep you around at least until our one-year anniversary. You have to be alive and healthy or you won't get your present, and that includes your birthday, too. So I'll see you tonight then, as soon as I'm through with work?"

After hanging up, Kayla mused, *One year. A year filled with moments of hurt but also of joy. It had been like climbing over boulders for occasional glimpses of a breathtaking waterfall.*

Marta arrived at Aunt Maggie's on time. She parked her van on the side of the road and lumbered over. She walked a lot like her dad. She wore jeans, a fleece jacket, and at her waist was a sheathed hunting knife. Kayla supposed it was a good idea to take a knife along when hauling horses in case they got a rope around their neck or leg in the trailer, but the size of this knife was unsettling.

They had the tack and Sundance loaded by ten, but when Taffy looked at the enclosed space, he planted his feet and refused to step into the trailer. After trying to coax him in for several minutes, Kayla sighed. "Aunt Maggie told me he was a bear to load. I wish I'd asked her how she finally managed it."

"My Arabian was a stubborn loader," Marta said. "I finally hooked a chain through her halter and over her nose. I only had to yank on that thing once to let her know I wasn't playing games. She gave up pronto and stepped into the trailer. Anytime she gave me trouble loading after that, all I had to do was rattle that chain. She couldn't get inside fast enough."

"Using a long whip will probably be enough for Taffy," Kayla said quickly. She sure didn't want to risk cutting up Taffy's nose or hurting him.

"I saw one inside," Marta said. "I'll get it."

"Just tap her," Kayla called when Marta returned. Marta gave a hard tap on Taffy's rear and the horse laid back his ears but refused to move forward. The second time Marta snapped the whip on Taffy's rear, his eyes rolled back, showing the whites. He was mad. With the third crack, he looked toward the whip, the trailer, and finally the whip again. He stepped in.

Kayla was grateful they were on their way, but she wondered if Marta had learned her forceful methods from her father.

By the time they'd driven for half an hour, Marta still hadn't mentioned her father's aggressive behavior toward Kayla. *Why didn't she apologize for him or make excuses? Why say nothing? Because she was equally involved?*

They talked about neutral subjects, pointing out returning sandhill cranes, geese, and turkey vultures. Kayla commented on the red-winged blackbirds staking out their territory and Marta spotted bags hanging from maple trees. "My dad used to do some maple sugaring."

"Oh?" Maybe if she encouraged Marta to talk about her father, she might let something slip.

"Yes. His family came over from Norway when he was eight. They had a small plot of land and eventually developed it into quite a farm. I know my father comes off as being gruff. Part of that is the way he was raised. He's quite a softy underneath, but that side doesn't show much."

"I've been wanting to talk to you about something," Kayla said, her throat tightening as she chewed on her lower lip. "Your mom seems quite confused. I know it isn't any of my business—"

"You're right," Marta said bluntly. "It's not."

Kayla felt as if she'd been slapped. She squared her shoulders. If Daisy was being abused, it was so her business. They rode in silence awhile before Marta must have decided she'd been too harsh and leaned toward her. "Just wait until you see these pictographs." As before, her voice became animated as she talked about them. "There's a hand print, a deer, and an abstract figure. We'll ride on the flood plain. There will be a gorgeous ridge on our left, and the river on our right. Once we're at the falls, we'll take the side road up to the ridge then to the pictograph canyon. You're going to love it."

There were several other cars in the parking lot. Taffy backed out of the trailer as soon as he was unhooked. Sundance was more cautious and concerned herself with looking around. Marta had Taffy tacked and ready as quickly as Kayla had Sundance. Marta mounted Taffy, then led the way down a rock-strewn hill to the sandy flood plain. The swiftly flowing river ran alongside, occasionally bubbling up when a boulder blocked its path. Several hikers dotted the landscape. "This is lovely," Kayla said.

"I knew you'd like it." Marta looked pleased. "I'm glad the water isn't any higher. I worried with the snow melting that it might be treacherous."

It was treacherous in spots as icy patches and uneven ground made for a challenging ride. They continued until Kayla came alongside Marta and asked, "Is that roaring sound the falls?"

"Yes. Hey, look behind us! Kayakers." Marta pointed. A man and a woman paddled red kayaks toward shore. "I'd say they miscalculated the current. I hope they make it in. They'd never survive if they were swept over those falls."

Fear flashed through Kayla. Even from this distance, Kayla could see they were concentrating on their strokes, pulling with all their strength. They muscled their way in, and when they reached shore, just yards from the growing turbulence, the man let out a whoop.

"Whew!" Kayla said. "That was too close for me."

"I need a cigarette myself," Marta said. "Let's stop a minute." Kayla came alongside. "Do you smoke?" Marta asked.

"No." While Marta lit up, the memory of Daisy's arm burned its way back into Kayla's thoughts.

Marta puffed away. "Except for loading," she said patting Taffy's neck, "I like this guy." Marta took another long drag, then blew the smoke from her mouth. "I've tried to quit," she said, staring at the cigarette. "My father calculated that he's spent $18,000 on cigarettes and all he has to show for it is lung problems, yellow teeth, and bad breath." She looked at the cigarette. "Maybe someday I'll be able to throw these away."

Kayla said, "Last time Rob and I went out to eat, we sat near a man in a wheelchair. He was hooked to an oxygen tank and had a package of cigarettes sticking out of his pocket."

"I believe it," Marta said, stroking the cigarette. "They can be your dearest friend."

Imagine having your dearest friend empty your wallet and kill you in the bargain! Hoping to swing the conversation back to Daisy, Kayla asked, "Your mom smokes, too, doesn't she?"

"Yes." Marta's tone sent sandpaper prickles down Kayla's spine. "I just want you to know one thing. My father takes good care of Mom. And that's not an easy job." Marta's face hardened. "There's a lot you don't know about my mother." Her words echoed against the rock ridge. Tossing her glowing stub into a patch of snow, she said, "We better keep going."

The next time Marta spoke she had to yell to be heard over the roar of the falls. "Our path to the pictographs is up here to the left. I need to use the outhouse just up the hill. How about you?"

"I'm fine," Kayla yelled back. "But I can hold Taffy."

"That's all right, there's a rail I can tie him to. Why don't you stay and look at the falls from that really great lookout point?"

"Over there?" Kayla pointed to the piece of land jutting out over the falls.

"Yes. Be careful though. It looks like the fence is down."

Marta and Taffy started ascending while Kayla crept closer to the edge. She still couldn't see the falls and took a few more steps. She wouldn't do this on any horse but Sundance. All it would take was one misstep and they could plummet over the brink. She'd once seen film footage of a horse somersaulting off a cliff and splashing into a lake.

One more step and the scene revealed itself. *How wonderful!* The icy blue water boiled and foamed over huge boulders until it darkened, resembling a root beer float. The power and pulse of the water were mesmerizing. She stared at it a long time. A flash of red made her wonder if someone was foolish enough to be kayaking in such turbulent water. She signaled Sundance to take two more steps closer to the edge so she could see. The rushing, swirling water sent a sudden wave of dizziness over her though, and she quickly signaled Sundance to back up.

At that moment a thundering sound drew her eyes upward toward the outhouse. An avalanche of rocks was crashing down from the ridge, heading straight toward them!

CHAPTER 6

Flirting with Danger

Hurry! Going to spook Sundance over the edge—into the falls. Here they come!

The tumbling, flying, ricocheting rocks were almost on them. "Turn around! Now!" Kayla yanked on the reins and pushed her leg into Sundance's side trying to get her to swing left. Sundance was too spooked to listen, though, and snorted and pranced frantically in place—thrashing her head back and forth. Kayla booted again, this time harder. Sundance's ears flicked back and forth from the descending rocks to the roaring falls. Another kick. Sundance reared up. *Hang on! Too close to the edge.* Sundance landed and planted her feet. *Should I jump off or keep trying to guide Sundance away?*

Sundance threw back her head again and snorted. Smaller rocks hit the mare's legs. She stumbled forward, a step closer to the edge, to the falls and the rocks below. Every nerve in Kayla's body wanted to scream, but Sundance needed her to be in control. "Steady now. Swing around." She held the reins to the left and kicked. But as another stream of rocks hit Sundance's legs, the mare crow-hopped, not wanting to go toward the rocks and not wanting to go over the edge. Out of the corner of her eye, Kayla caught sight of a huge, jagged rock. It ricocheted off a tree and now crashed down the hill toward them. In seconds it could swipe them off the edge.

"This way!" Kayla forced Sundance's head around and booted again. With the leap of a wildcat, Sundance suddenly bounded toward the ridge, the jagged end of the huge rock just missing her hind legs. Another leap, and another. The sound of the rocks crashing onto the ground far below them thundered in Kayla's ears, and then there was silence. Silence, except for Kayla's own soft whimpers.

Kayla stumbled from her horse, and with her legs trembling, she sank to the ground. "Sundance," she mumbled feeling the mare's legs. *No blood. Broken bones?* Someone was saying something to Kayla, but there was only the roar of the falls in her ears. Her trembling hands still clutched the reins. "Can you walk?" She tugged gently. Sundance stepped ahead without a limp. "Thank God." Kayla sank onto the ground, and a young woman dressed in hiking clothes took the reins from her.

"Are you all right?" the woman asked in a voice that could barely be heard over the falls. Her face was so pale and frightened that Kayla forced herself to respond.

"I'm okay." But Kayla's voice cracked. Looking at Sundance, she repeated, "We're okay."

The young man who was with the woman said, "I didn't see how it started." He looked toward the ridge and pointed at Marta hurrying toward them. "Maybe this woman did."

Marta was hurrying down the hill.

"Kayla!" Marta exclaimed, arriving at Kayla's side. "My God! You were nearly plowed over!"

The young man asked, "Did you see what happened?"

"No, I didn't see anything." Marta's gaze shifted, and Kayla noticed her neck had red blotches just like when she'd said that Daisy had burned herself on the oven. *Do the blotches appear when she tells a lie?* Kayla stared at her dumbly, letting the thought sink in.

Finally Marta asked, "How badly is Sundance hurt?"

"She...she seems to be okay," Kayla said, "but—" she took several deep breaths, "but I don't want to go any farther." Kayla thanked the girl hiker then took back the reins. Still watching her horse carefully, Kayla said, "I'll walk her back to the parking lot."

As Kayla led Sundance and Marta rode Taffy back along the river, Marta said, "I'm so sorry about this, Kayla. Who would have thought something like that could happen? I've never heard of rock slides out here, but of course there are a lot of rocks. I had just gotten done in the outhouse and was about to untie Taffy when I heard the crashing sound. Then, when I saw you and Sundance at the edge, I screamed. My heart jumped into my throat when she wouldn't move. I thought for sure you two were going over."

Marta kept the prattle up all the way back to the trailer. *Was she nervous because of what almost happened, or for another reason?*

Fortunately, Taffy loaded easily. After the trailer was secured, Marta asked, "Would you rather I drive?"

Even though she was still shaky, Kayla knew she would feel better if she were in control of the pickup and trailer. "No, I'll be okay."

Marta made some attempts at conversation on the way back, but Kayla could only give short answers. Finally, they arrived at Aunt Maggie's. Marta helped Kayla unload, return the horses to the pasture, and clean up the trailer. Then, with a final apology, she left.

As her car pulled away, Kayla stared after her. *Would keeping her abusive father's secret be so important to Marta that she'd actually start an avalanche and try to kill me? What kind of hold did Marta's father have over her? No. That rock slide had to have started by itself. But yet...* Kayla shook her head in bewilderment as she headed for her own home.

A few minutes later she was opening the front door. The empty house closed in around Kayla, and every creaking heater or wind noise made her cringe. She wished she could call Rob at work, but her story could wait. Finally she called Josie and thankfully found her at home. "Can I stop by for a few minutes?"

"Sure, come on over."

Josie couldn't make sense of it either after Kayla poured out the details of the grueling day. Kayla kept calm until she'd answered most of Josie's questions, but when Josie asked her once again if she thought Marta had pushed a rock and started the rock slide, Kayla sucked in her breath. The enormity of it was too much to imagine. "I suppose it's possible," she finally said. Then, as if the waterfall of her pent emotions couldn't be held back any longer, she shook with sobs. Josie put her arm around her friend and let her cry. Finally, after she was spent, Kayla said, "I'm sorry."

"Hey, it's good you got it out. I wish I knew how to help, though." Josie ran her fingers through her hair, making it look wilder than ever. "I think you should tell your parents—"

"No." Kayla's back instantly straightened. "You know how they'd react."

"Well, at least let me call Rob."

Kayla looked at her watch. "He's just finishing work," Kayla said, a final sob escaping. "I'm supposed to meet him now. Thanks for talking things through with me."

"You sure you're all right to drive back?"

"I'm okay."

○ ○ ○

When Rob's jeep pulled up, she did feel better. She saw by Rob's stiff back and tight jaw muscles, though, that something was wrong with him. "What is it?" she asked.

"We need to talk."

Kayla sat on the sofa, but Rob chose a chair. "Tracy asked me today if we'd broken up. She said she was at the Holiday Inn on Thursday and you were there with a man. I figured she was mistaken and asked what you were wearing. She said a black lacy top."

"I was there...with Dr. Nerad." She couldn't look at him.

"With Dr. Nerad?" Rob's sharp tone cut like jagged glass.

"It was innocent enough."

"Why didn't you tell me, then? Why did I have to find out from my boss's daughter?"

Kayla let out a long breath. "Because I knew you'd act like this. Because I didn't want to justify it to you or argue about it."

"I thought our relationship was based on trust. Trust includes being honest. I don't call this honest."

"Rob," Kayla said, holding her head, "could we talk about this later?"

"I need some answers, Kayla. Are you flirting with this guy?"

"No! I can't believe you'd ask me that."

"Why were you dressed like that then, and why hadn't you told me you were meeting him?"

"I didn't know. I'd been working in his office and he asked me to go with him for coffee."

"Wearing a black lacy top? Late at night? To a hotel?"

"To a restaurant."

Rob sighed. "Kayla, this guy is a jerk, plain and simple! Am I right?"

Kayla stiffened. She would have liked to confide her suspicions about Nerad to Rob, but when he acted like this, she just wanted to prove him wrong. When she didn't answer he continued. "What did you talk about?"

"Career options." Kayla wasn't about to say anything about her sense of unease. What she wanted right now was sympathy, not criticism. Rob hadn't even given her a chance to tell him about Marta and the rock slide. Fearing her eyes would soon well up with tears, she quickly said, "You ought to go now. It's late and I'm tired." She stood up.

"Kayla," he said, facing her and clasping both her hands, "don't do this to us. I'm sorry I attacked you. I was upset—"

"I was upset today, too," Kayla began. "At the falls, at a steep place, an avalanche of rocks spooked Sundance. They came straight toward us—"

Rob's grip tightened. "What happened?"

Now her eyes did well up with tears. "We were near the edge—I was so afraid."

Rob held her tight. "Oh, honey, I didn't know. A rock slide? What caused it?"

"Nothing that anyone saw, but, Rob?" Kayla could barely form the words as she looked at him. "Marta was up on top of the ridge when it happened. I don't want to believe she caused it, but I just don't know."

Rob shook his head. "This is so bizarre. Do you think she set out to hurt you because you know her dad is abusive?"

Kayla shrugged. "Maybe Marta is afraid the police are going to haul him off to jail."

Rob asked, "But why isn't she just as protective of her mother?"

"I don't know." Kayla thought of Daisy's bruise and formed a mental image of Marta's powerful hands. Should she say what she was thinking? Yes, she could tell Rob. "The thought has even occurred to me that it might not be Rottweiler who gave Daisy the burn and bruise. Maybe it was...Marta."

Rob asked, "Did you call the police?"

"No, but I'm going to be very careful when she's around."

"You aren't thinking of going back there, are you?"

"Last time I left Daisy with her husband and daughter she had a bruise and cigarette burn. I don't know what I can do, but I know I can't abandon her."

Rob held her away from him so he could look at her. "You need to take care of yourself, too." They held each other and talked until past midnight. Finally, Rob kissed her, then softly stroked her cheek. "You look tired. I better let you get to bed. Are you going to be all right?"

"Yes," she said, but as she locked the door behind him, she felt a spasm of fear shoot through her body. A car drove by. She peered out the window. *A sports car. Not Marta's van. Of course she could be using someone else's car.* For a moment she thought of Luke, the man with obsessive-compulsive tendencies who had pursued her over the winter. He'd driven a sports car, but why would he start shadowing her now? Feeling as if her world was spinning backwards, Kayla quickly moved to check all the doors and windows.

She lay in bed for a long time listening to the house creak and moan before she fell asleep. Sometime after one o'clock she awoke abruptly. Had she been having a nightmare about the rock avalanche and falling off the edge? Was the noise she heard real or in her head? *There it is again! Footsteps. Someone is inside the house.* Kayla's heart beat double time as she strained to listen. *Luke? Marta or Rottweiler? Are Marta and her father back to finish the job?* As the footsteps came closer, Kayla looked for a weapon on her nightstand. *A picture frame. If I hit the intruder hard enough in the throat with a sharp corner, I'd have enough time to get away.*

The steps paused outside her bedroom door. Every muscle in her body tensed. *Please don't come in. Please don't come in,* she wished. Her bedroom door creaked open, and a silhouette appeared. *Marta, hunting knife in hand?*

"Kayla?"

The figure stepped closer. "Dad!"

"Hi, honey, sorry to wake you."

"You scared me half to death." Kayla rose, hand to her chest, and turned on a lamp. "What...why are you home?"

"I was on stand-by and got a late flight. Sorry I didn't have time to call."

"Grandpa?" Kayla asked, catching her breath.

"No change." Dad looked bone weary. "So, how are things going here?"

"Uh...okay. Everything's fine. When will Mom come home?"

"It may be a while." He sat beside her, patting her hand, his voice slow and soft. "The doctors have warned us that Grandma's blood pressure is way up and Grandpa—well, he could go at any time. Mom's hoping to make it home Wednesday for your birthday, but I don't know."

"I hope she's not worrying about me. We'll just celebrate my birthday later."

Dad nodded. "I'll let you get back to sleep. We can talk tomorrow." Dad hesitated and Kayla had the feeling he wanted a hug. She put her arms out. He quickly moved forward and wrapped her in his arms.

After he'd left, Kayla was glad she'd given him the hug. A person never knew when life would end, and it made sense to live each moment to the fullest.

CHAPTER 7

Birthday Basket Overflowing with Dreams

Four days later, Grandpa was still comatose. Dad sat down with Kayla. "Your mother and aunt are being torn in half. They want to be with Grandma and Grandpa, but they hate being away from home." He sighed. "Oh, and I talked to Uncle Jim. He'll be flying in tonight, and I'm going to pick him up. All four of the eggs he took over hatched and the chicks are thriving. The Russians are pleased."

Kayla was pleased, too. Having Uncle Jim back would relieve her of some of her farm chores. She needed the extra time to study, especially for the history midterm.

Wednesday morning, Dad made her a pancake birthday breakfast. After cleaning up, he began, "How about—" but the phone interrupted his question.

"It's Rob," she explained to Dad.

"Talk to you later." Dad waved and left for work.

"So," Rob asked, "how's your birthday so far?"

"So far so good, but maybe I ought to delay that answer until after I take my midterm."

"You'll do well. I know you. See you in the library later?"

"All right." With the house quiet, Kayla settled down to study. When her mind was drawn to Nerad, or the unsolved mystery of Daisy's bruise and burn mark, she forced herself to refocus on the Civil War. Finally, it was time to leave for work.

Kayla found Josie at the museum visiting with Cody. "Hey, Birthday Girl," she said. "I hung around to see how you're doing."

"I'm doing okay."

"Want to open your presents?" Josie asked, handing her a small Ho-Chunk basket. "The basket's from Cody."

Kayla drew in her breath. The fawn-colored basket with red and yellow trim had been one she'd admired. She often explained to customers all the work involved: from finding just the right black ash, to the cutting, pounding, separating of the annual rings, and finally the dyeing and assembly. "Thank you, Cody, but this is much too extravagant a gift."

Cody grinned and shook his head. "You know," he said, "baskets were originally designed to hold the dreams of the Ho-Chunk Nation." Kayla thought of the huge basket that'd be needed to hold all her dreams: for Grandpa to get well, for Rob and her to continue to grow closer, for Daisy to be safe from harm, and for Nerad to act like a real professor and not ask questions that made her feel uneasy and suspicious.

Josie said, "The gift inside is from me."

The turquoise earrings had specks of brown mixed in with the bluish stone. "These are beautiful. Thanks, Josie, you know exactly what I like."

"Let's talk after class, okay?"

Kayla nodded.

After they'd left, she looked at the schedule. A one o'clock tour of ten people was listed. Being a tour guide was a promotion of sorts. She preferred it over clerking or stocking shelves and after listening to Cody so many times, she was able to do it easily.

Today the group was rather quiet and asked few questions. A plain-looking woman, tall and thin, was quietest of all. Afterwards, she thanked Kayla for the tour and introduced herself as the dean of Nicolet College. "Oh," Kayla said, "I go to school there."

The dean reached out and shook her hand. "And what is your name?"

"Kayla Montgomery. I'm a freshman with several possible majors yet." She smiled sheepishly.

"Well, if you ever need anything, stop by my office."

Kayla watched long after she'd left. She'd never have put this timid-appearing woman in the role of a college dean. Then Kayla thought again. She hadn't been vocal because she'd been listening to Kayla. Listening would be a great characteristic for a dean, and now that Kayla looked at her differently, she bet the woman could speak with authority if she felt strongly about an issue. First impressions, Kayla realized, were sometimes wrong.

A while later, after deciding on a turquoise necklace, an older man handed Kayla a check. Kayla glanced down the names on the "no checks accepted" list. *Marta Erickson-Henry!* That's where she'd seen the name Marta! Long after she completed the transaction, her mind churned with the thought that Marta wrote bad checks. *How desperate was she for money?*

Kayla's mind was kept occupied with the discovery about Marta, work, and her Native American culture class, so she didn't have a chance to get nervous about the mid-term until she walked into Nerad's class. Remembering his low-voiced statement, "you don't need to worry about the midterm," she flushed. But thank heaven he handed her a blue book and test questions showing no indication that she was any different from any of his other students.

The test had seven essay questions. *Shoot,* Kayla thought. *I hoped there would be multiple choice or short answer.* But she forged ahead with the first one: Where in America did urbanization and industrialization lead to greater class structure between the end of the Revolution and the Civil War? Kayla took a deep breath, pictured the Ho-chunk basket of dreams and began.

"That's time," Dr. Nerad said, an hour later.

She finished her thought on the last question then filed forward with her classmates. As she handed her test to Nerad, she smiled, sure she'd done well.

He smiled back. "Wait here," he said in a low voice.

Kayla stepped away, letting the others turn in their tests. She hoped Nerad hadn't misinterpreted her smile. It had been a smile of relief that she'd done a fair job on the test, nothing more.

When they were alone, Nerad's voice was professional and his sentences ended on the upbeat as if he was lecturing in class. "Kayla, I'm wondering if you'd be interested in helping me with a project this spring. I've been asked to coordinate the community event celebrating the state's sesquicentennial, May 29th. Arrangements are being made to have a community picture taken and a celebration at Heritage Park that Saturday. I'm coordinating some local crafters, quilters and weavers, and there'll also be some reenactors: a Revolutionary War soldier, a surgeon, and we hope to have a pioneer teacher and some students. A woman with a team of Percherons has offered to bring the school children in by wagon."

"Sounds like a great idea," Kayla said.

"I was wondering if you'd be willing to be the teacher." The image of having to work with Nerad flashed through Kayla's mind and she wanted to say no. "There are people who could help you find a costume, and I know from your writings that you can ride."

"But not sidesaddle," she said, hoping to make a light joke and gently dissuade him.

Dr. Nerad smiled. "I promise not to turn you in for inaccuracy. You'd make an impressive sight." Kayla pictured herself in a blue calico dress, high-button shoes, and bonnet trotting up to the park on Sundance. It would be a great way to celebrate the state's one hundred-fiftieth birthday.

"How about it?" he asked again.

"It does sound like fun."

Dr. Nerad leaned closer. "We could discuss whether you'd like to teach a lesson or have the kids play old-fashioned games, then have a taffy pull. So you'll do it?"

"I... I guess I could."

"Great. Now for a special favor," Dr. Nerad said, hanging his head slightly. "I'm a terrible procrastinator and I've been especially bad on this project. The committee meets tomorrow afternoon, so would you help me work out the details tonight?"

Kayla's instincts buzzed red alert. She asked, "Who all is involved?"

"It would just be you and me. We could go to the Holiday Inn or another restaurant if you'd prefer. It shouldn't take us long."

She wasn't keen on meeting him in the evening again, her birthday of all nights. But Dad hadn't mentioned doing anything and Rob hadn't set up a time to stop over, though she was sure he expected to.

Dr. Nerad asked again, "Tonight's all right then?"

Kayla nodded.

"Eight-thirty? We can meet here at school."

Kayla nodded once more.

As she hurried to meet Rob at the library, she realized the full impact of what she'd done. Why couldn't she have simply said *No?* Because she couldn't stand up to him, she realized. The terms professor, noted author, and doctor intimidated her. And, she also realized, he had cleverly ordered and stated his questions so it was easier to say yes than no. If he'd begun with, Will you meet me at the hotel tonight? she would have quickly said *No*. But he'd gotten her to agree to the project and once that was accomplished, it followed that they'd need to meet.

Kayla went to the isolated library table she and Rob thought of as theirs, and found Rob flipping through a magazine.

"Hey, that didn't take too long."

"Long enough, but I think I did okay. On the exam," she added as an afterthought. She sat down across from him.

"Now you can relax and have a good time tonight. I thought I'd take you to Fantasy Gardens. They have their orchids and lilies—"

"Rob," she said quickly, hoping to get this over with. "I told Dr. Nerad I'd go over a few things with him tonight at 8:30—"

"You what? On your birthday?" Rob looked around. The place was nearly empty but a few students were studying. He took a deep breath. "What's going on, Kayla?"

"He wants me to help with the sesquicentennial celebration May 29th and we need to meet tonight—"

"For a celebration that's two and a half months away?"

"But the committee meeting is tomorrow afternoon."

"Kayla," Rob said covering her hand. "Your father just got home and today is your birthday. Do you really want to spend the evening with Nerad?"

"No," she admitted, "I don't." She wasn't about to admit to how she'd been maneuvered, but she did confess, "Only I don't know how to get out of it."

"Call him up and tell him you can't make it, simple as that!"

Simple? Calling a college professor at home? Later, her heart seemed to be beating 1000 times a minute as a pleasant-sounding voice answered, "Nerad's, Clarisse speaking."

"Hello, may I speak to Dr. Nerad?"

"Certainly." Mrs. Nerad sounded young and Kayla had a hard time picturing the unhealthy, unattractive woman Nerad had described.

"Hello?"

"Dr. Nerad, this is Kayla. I'm sorry, but I can't make it tonight. It's my birthday and my family has planned something." The words came out in a rush and Kayla found

103

she'd been gripping the phone so hard her knuckles were white.

"I see, we'll have to talk after class sometime." Click.

That was all. *Why the sudden hangup? Is he upset? Does he mind I called him at home?*

○ ○ ○

Kayla tried not to think about it as she, Dad, and Rob celebrated her birthday. Afterward, they sat in the living room to open gifts. Dad handed her a glittery card with images of stuffed animals and spinning CDs. It was a card appropriate for a young girl, not a college student. "Mom usually picks out the cards," Dad said sheepishly.

Kayla smiled, "It's fine, Dad." She opened it up and a catalog tire picture fluttered out.

"Your car needs a new set," Dad said. "I'll take it in this week. Mom has a few other gifts for you to open."

"Thanks, this is great," Kayla said giving him a big hug. He held her a second longer than expected. She was glad she'd canceled her meeting with Nerad.

The first gift she unwrapped from Rob was a tiger emblem for her karate uniform. Rob said, "They had others, but when I asked your instructor which would be best, he said, 'The tiger. Tigers represent strength and tenacity, and if I'm reading Kayla right, she has both.'"

He also gave her a lemon yellow dress. "It reminds me of the color of the first dress I saw you in," Rob said. "I thought you could wear it on our one-year anniversary date. It won't be long now."

"It's beautiful—thanks, honey."

The final gift was a turquoise and silver horseshoe necklace. "Josie told me about the Ho-Chunk basket and turquoise earrings. I thought this would match and bring you good luck besides."

As he fastened it around her neck, she thought, *I could use a little of that.*

CHAPTER 8

Obscure Pictographs

Thursday afternoon, Kayla paced the house. It had been a week since she'd taken Daisy for the horseback ride and had been the victim of Rottweiler's verbal abuse. Did she dare ride out there again? No, Rottweiler would be expecting her. But what if Daisy needed her? "I know!" she said aloud.

She tucked her hair up under a knit hat and grabbed her coat. Ten minutes later she was outside The Corner Cafe. If he was there and recognized her, she'd simply pretend she had stopped for something to eat. Several snowmobiles dotted the parking lot. Not being sure which would be Rottweiler's, she had to go in.

Four older men sat around a large table eating sandwiches and drinking coffee. Two of the men had beards and two wore flannel shirts like Rottweiler's. Kayla was sure this was the group. Rottweiler must be staying with Daisy in case she showed up again.

As she drove home, Kayla wondered how long it would take before he'd rejoin his buddies. If only there were some way to know if Marta could be trusted. *But there is!* Kayla's mind whirled. *Or at least there's a way to find out if she's a liar. If I go back to Painted Falls and find there aren't any pictographs, I'll know Marta lied. Maybe the pictographs were just an excuse to get me on the trail where she could cause an accident. It's possible she scoped out the terrain and even planned where she'd want me standing when she started the rock slide.*

Kayla left a message at the flower shop for Rob to call back. When he did, she explained about going to Painted Falls, then asked, "What do you think?"

"It's a great idea. Going to let me come with you?"

"Sure."

Rob frowned. "It does seem strange that no one knows about this place, at least I've never heard of it. I know it's not a state park, but still...to have rock art so close and never to have heard of it?"

The first day they could find a mutual chunk of time turned out to be a week from Saturday. Kayla was disappointed at the delay, but she didn't want to go alone and maybe having the time to think things through would turn out for the best. Still, it was hard to go so long without knowing what was happening to Daisy!

Kayla wasn't keen on riding the horses there again, especially since Rob wasn't that great a rider, so they decided to hike in. "It'll be a long walk," Kayla warned Rob, "but next week's supposed to be warm."

○ ○ ○

The day before they were to go, Kayla called Rob and said, "My mom's coming home tomorrow, too, but she's taking a late plane, so we should be back from Painted Falls in time."

"And your grandpa?"

"No change. I could tell by Mom's voice that her nerves are shot." Kayla sighed. "Speaking of nerves," she said twirling the phone cord, " I get my history test back today."

An hour later, Kayla had substituted a lock of hair for the phone cord. She had it twisted into a knot by the time Nerad handed her back her midterm. Her heart skipped a beat when a big, red D flamed at her. The comments included: "Needs more development. Unclear. Where is your proof?" She sat stunned while he gave final instructions for the next assignment, a research paper, also worth one-third of the final grade. After class he stopped her. "Kayla, could we go up to my office so I can check my calendar and we can reschedule our meeting time?"

"Sure." Kayla followed numbly, wondering why he wanted her to be a reenactor if he thought she was so inept at history.

"Have a seat," he said.

Kayla walked around a stack of books, set her midterm on the desk, then took off her backpack and sat across from him. The office was cluttered again. He smiled and with a shrug said, "I tried to keep it neat, but I'm incorrigible. I may have to hire you on a maintenance plan."

Kayla tried to smile back, but her heart was thumping too hard. Nerad studied a calendar. "I have commitments until next week Friday. Would that work?"

She would have preferred a time other than the weekend, but she nodded. He said, "You seem especially quiet. Are you upset about your grade?"

"Yes, I am."

"Don't worry. You'll be able to raise it, I'm sure. You still have your research paper and the final."

"I hope so. Otherwise this is going to look awful on my transcript to say nothing of what it'll do to my GPA."

"Kayla?" When Kayla heard the same husky tone he'd used when saying she didn't need to study for the midterm, every muscle in her body tightened. "There may be a way to earn some extra credit."

Kayla's mouth went dry. Her stomach rolled. "Like what?"

He didn't answer. Instead, he raised his eyebrows and leered at her. Then he stepped closer. She quickly stood, then backed up until she hit the wall. She held her backpack in front of her. Bile rose to her throat. *This must be how Daisy felt when she was trapped.* It seemed absurd to be thinking of Daisy at a time like this, but with Nerad's face only inches from her own, she silently said, *Be strong, like I want Daisy to be strong. Find the tiger in myself.*

"I don't like what you're implying." She had tried to growl it out, but it came out more like a mew.

"And what am I implying?" Now his hand reached for her thigh.

"You're...sick. I... I ought to report you for this." She slid toward the door but Nerad stepped in front of her.

"For what?"

"You know for what."

"No I don't."

"Sexual harassment! Selling grades for sex."

"You're crazy!"

Hackles raised, Kayla stepped past him and grabbed the doorknob. "I could report this to the dean. Your students and your wife will find out and you'll be humiliated in front of this entire college."

"You do that and I'll tell about your provocative dress—"

"My *what?*" Kayla looked down at her sweatshirt and jeans.

"The black lacy top you wore last week. Our waitress will remember, I'm sure."

Kayla felt like she was going to be sick. How this would humiliate her, to say nothing of her parents!

"The fact is you've been coming on to me all semester, showing up at my office at odd hours. Won't people enjoy hearing about that?" She had the door open when Nerad, in a voice so soft she barely heard, spat out, "You really think anyone is going to believe you?"

She hurried down the hallway, his hateful words echoing in her head. She stumbled into her car, but when her hand shook too much to get the key in the ignition, she covered her face, feeling like a helpless grub trying to hide from a hungry mole. She pushed back her tears and her panic and uncovered her face. Rob had tried to help her, but it was clear she had to do this on her own. She needed to think things through.

If she reported him, maybe the dean would ask another professor to grade her test. That person was certain to disagree with Nerad. Her exam! She'd left it on the creep's desk! It was her proof! She lay her head on the steering wheel in despair. Then, she remembered the office key. She still had it! She'd ask Rob to come back with her later.

As she started the car, Nerad's parting words burned their way into her skull: You really think anyone is going to believe you? An experienced history professor, noted author, a doctor, and the recipient of the Chancellor's Award for Excellence vs. a freshman. She wouldn't stand a chance.

Rob. She needed to talk to Rob. She had been less than honest with him, and it was time to confess. Kayla drove to the flower shop, but his delivery van was gone. She waited in her car for half an hour before she saw him drive up. He came hurrying over. "Kayla?"

"I need to talk to you, Rob."

"All right. Let me tell my boss. We're through for the night anyway."

When he returned she asked, "Can we drive back to the college?"

"Sure." The fact that he didn't ask why, just led her to his yellow jeep and drove off, gave Kayla hope.

"You were right, Rob. Nerad came on to me again."

"Again?"

"Yes, the first time I wasn't sure. He made a comment about my not needing to worry about the midterm. It made my skin crawl, but I didn't know if I was reading it right. After tonight, I'm sure."

"What did he do?" The vein in Rob's neck bulged.

"He gave me a D on my midterm then..." Kayla felt heat rise to her cheeks, "then suggested there was a way to earn extra credit."

Rob's eyes riveted on her. "That—"

"Rob! A car!"

Rob swerved back in his lane and slowed down. "I knew he was a pervert!" he shouted. "A slimy, creepy pervert."

"Rob, slow down. You're going too fast again."

Rob braked, but his fingers still clenched the steering wheel.

"I wanted to go back to his office because I left my midterm on his desk. I thought it might be needed for evidence."

"Evidence?"

"If I have to file charges on him, they'll want to see the midterm."

"Of course," Rob said, furrowing his brow. "They could look at it and see if he graded it unfairly. Do you still have the key?"

"Yes, I do. I didn't want to go back alone. Thanks for bringing me."

"Kayla?" Rob said, his voice hollow.

Kayla knew what he was going to say. She tried to explain. "I know I hadn't told you the whole story, Rob, but I hoped my instincts were wrong."

Rob stopped for a light and looked at her. "If we're going to have a lifelong relationship, we need to be honest with each other." The light turned green but he didn't step on the gas. When a horn blared, Rob ignored it. "I'm no philosopher, but the way I figure, life is full of tangled mazes and in order to get through, we need to grab each other by the hand and pull together. That's how we find the way."

Kayla covered his hand with hers. "You're right. I wish I'd listened to you and never gotten into this mess." Kayla groaned. "Now I might have to file charges and I can't imagine having to tell my parents. Even if he's proven to be at fault, my name will be spread around like manure. Oh, I hope that test is still there."

Half an hour later, Rob and Kayla crept down the dark halls, opened the office door, and flipped on the light. They searched, but the midterm was gone.

○ ◯ ○

How do I get into these messes? Kayla asked herself after Rob dropped her off. The situation with Nerad was one problem she surely didn't need. If she decided to file sexual harassment charges, she'd have to tell her parents. They'd ask questions and some of the answers she'd give would be embarrassing. It was a fact she'd gone out with the professor to a hotel restaurant and that she'd worn a black lacy top. A woman should be allowed to wear what she wanted without worrying about being harassed, but Kayla knew some people would think she'd asked for it. Nerad would also surely tell she'd gone to his office at odd hours, insinuating that she wanted to meet him. Would her parents think she'd encouraged him?

Before she told them, she'd do some research. Rob and she had discussed finding out the track record of other young women who had filed so she'd know what she was up against. The library would have court cases and information.

When her mom and Aunt Maggie called a few minutes later, it was all Kayla could do to sound normal. Only knowing how stressed out they were that Grandpa hadn't improved stopped her from leaning on them for support. Dad talked quite a while then called, "Kayla, could you come in here for a minute?"

Was it Grandpa? What hadn't Mom and Aunt Maggie told her?

"What is it?" she asked.

"It's about Joey."

"Oh, you scared me. I thought they were thinking of giving up on Grandpa."

"No, although if that has to happen, it will be very hard, but Grandpa has lived a full life. Joey, on the other hand, hasn't."

"So what's up with Joey?"

"The doctor's expect his grandma to recover from the stroke, but she may need help caring for Joey."

"Are you saying you're thinking of letting Joey stay here once in a while? Kind of like the big sisters program?"

"Yes. Joey will be with the Coopers, a foster family, until his grandma is better. His grandma is concerned that she won't be able to take him places much. That's where we come in. Trips to the zoo, a camp out, the museum, whatever we'd like to do."

Kayla's head swam with scenes of carving pumpkins, nature walks, and maybe a weekend at a cabin on a lake. The romantic images faded quickly, however, when she remembered Joey's poor behavior. As if Dad read her thoughts, he said, "Joey's a troubled boy, there's no doubt about that, but underneath there's also a loving, tender child. Together we might be able to bring some of that out. It's nothing you have to decide now. But Mom and I would like to try it and we'd like you to think about it. Joey has had so much disruption in his life, we don't want to start this if we're not serious about seeing it through."

"I will think about it, Dad."

"Fair enough," Dad said.

"I'm off to work on my history paper now," Kayla said. "I want to do well on it."

"All right, honey," Dad said.

Thoughts of Joey came to mind throughout the weekend as Kayla worked and reworked her history paper, perfecting it so Nerad wouldn't have an excuse to fail her. By Monday morning, she was confident she was well on her way to an A paper.

During history class, Nerad switched from ignoring her to pouncing on her with difficult questions. Not often enough to be termed harassing, but enough to make her uncomfortable.

As soon as class was dismissed, she hurried to the library where she requested several publications on sexual harassment. She gave a great sigh; *the grub just might escape the mole after all.*

On Wednesday, she had to face him again. As she handed him her completed research paper, the mole wore a triumphant half-smile. He was confident, licking his lips, enjoying taunting her.

Kayla thought about describing his expression for Rob on their way to see the pictographs on Saturday, but found out he'd seen it himself. "I went in yesterday," Rob began.

"You what!"

"I would have told you, but it was a sudden decision. What he's been doing to you has been eating away at me and I just had to confront him."

"What happened?"

"He played dumb, claiming he didn't know what I was talking about. Thought I might be overreacting as a jealous boyfriend. He was Mr. Suave and brushed me off like dandruff."

Kayla covered Rob's hand with hers. "Thanks for trying. Nerad sure fooled me. I hadn't expected him to be so clever and deceptive. It reminds me of that Bible verse: *Beware of false prophets, which come to you in sheep's clothing, but inwardly they are ravening wolves.*"

"He's a wolf all right. A clever, scheming, perverted wolf."

"And Marta may be no better," Kayla added. "She may very well have fooled me, too. If we don't find the pictographs, do you think the fact she lied to me is enough to convince the police to check things out?"

"It's worth a phone call," Rob said. "If she lied about the rock art, it's possible she planned all along to hurt you."

"And if she'd be willing to hurt me, she might be doing the same to her mother. I can't figure out what she stands to gain, though."

Rob asked, "Does Daisy have a lot of money?"

"I don't know."

"If she does, and she's not planning on leaving it to her husband or Marta, that might be a reason for them to drug her. If she's found incompetent, they could contest the will."

Kayla held her head. It was a horrid thought. She prayed it wasn't true, yet she thought of Marta's name on the "bad check" list.

Rob said, "I suppose there's another possibility. Maybe Marta's protecting her father and wants you out of the way because you know what he's like."

"By why would she protect her father and not her mother?"

Rob frowned. "I have no idea."

The Painted Falls parking lot had more cars than last time, and a few people were visible in the distance. Kayla took a deep breath and led the way toward the falls.

Rob held her hand as they hiked on the flood plain along the river. When they finally reached the place where she and Sundance had stood while the avalanche of rocks tumbled toward them and the edge, her grip on Rob's hand tightened. She described to Rob how Sundance had pranced about while the falling rocks hit her legs and the boulder had headed straight toward them.

Rob frowned. "If Marta pushed a big rock that started the others going when you were near the edge, she must have meant to seriously hurt you."

Kayla shuddered.

They turned down the path Marta had pointed out and walked for another thirty minutes, but there was no sign of pictographs. Rob sighed. "Think we should head back?"

"Just another ten minutes," Kayla said. She had so hoped to find the rock art. Thinking about having to call the police when they got home only made her pulse quicken. She'd have to tell them she thought Marta made up this elaborate story to lure her to this treacherous place. If there hadn't been a chance to start a rock slide toward Kayla, what would Marta have done instead?

As they came to a bend in the path, a beautiful bowl-shaped canyon with a waterfall made Kayla suck in her breath. Water cascaded down onto rock, then flowed into a stream. Rob whispered, "This is incredible."

Kayla said, "Can't you picture early people gathered here? I can almost hear their voices."

"There's a strong aura, all right." Rob stepped ahead. "We may find the pictographs yet." Kayla studied the rocks closely.

Rob called from the far end near the waterfall, "Here they are!"

Kayla hurried over. When she saw the faded red lines on the left, a deer in the center and a hand print on the right, a great sense of well-being overwhelmed her. She held her hand up to the other, measuring. They were the same size. She was stepping in the same spot where

119

someone her size had stepped hundreds of years ago. *Humankind continues. Antiquity. From time immemorial.*

"There's a sign explaining this," Rob said. "The color of the pictographs has faded from bold red or orange. The one on the left may represent a man in ceremonial dress portraying a vision he experienced."

Kayla could see how the figure of the man, attached by a thread of thought to another bird-like figure, could have that interpretation.

"And it says they used red ochre," Rob said, pointing to the information, "a mixture of rusted iron ore and bear grease or sturgeon oil, to make the paint."

Kayla took a step closer to study them. "Marta said they'd probably be faded in another fifty years." At the mention of Marta, Kayla realized this proved Marta hadn't lied. It didn't mean, of course, that she wasn't in cahoots with her father, or that she hadn't caused her mother's bruise or burn mark, or that she hadn't seized the opportunity to send the rock slide in Kayla's direction. In fact, Kayla realized with a sigh, she was no closer to solving this puzzle than she'd been two hours ago.

They stood in silence. Kayla imagined the presence of native people, echoes from the past. She pictured early people gathered in this bowl-shaped meeting room, surrounded by these protective rocks. Dark-haired children looked for tadpoles in the stream or tossed hoops in the air. Men played dice games or made arrowheads. Women visited each other as they scraped hides, watched the stew and kept track of the children. And possibly on the village outskirts, a young man mixed red ochre to make the drawings.

Kayla said, "Last week in my Native American class we had a speaker who ended the speech by asking, 'What is there to tie us to the people who have lived here before if we don't honor the Earth Spirit and take care of the land and its people?'"

It wasn't a question to be answered, but a question for the conscience. Long after they left the canyon, the words still echoed in Kayla's head. *Take care of the land and its people...people...*people.

CHAPTER 9

Voices From the Past

When Kayla got home that evening, her mom met her at the door. "Oh," Mom said, giving her a big hug, "it seems like months since I've seen you."

"I'm so glad you're back," Kayla said, hugging her tighter than she'd expected to.

Mom held her away, studying her. "Are you all right?"

"Yes. How's Grandpa doing?"

They sat down in the kitchen. "Still no change, but we found a wonderful, older woman to stay with Grandma. Shirley and Grandma knew each other when they were kids. Grandma likes her and she genuinely cares about Grandma."

"Is Aunt Maggie back, too?"

"Yes, she's hoping you'll stop over when you get a chance." Mom looked tired, but there was something else. Excitement? "Dad says he talked to you about Joey?" she asked.

"Yes." Kayla knew she wanted to know if including him in their family would be all right. *Take care of the land and its people.* "If you and Dad want to invite him over, it's fine with me."

"Good." Mom smiled and she looked almost happy.

Kayla said, "Maybe I could take him horseback riding some time."

"Oh, he'd love that."

"All right. I'll head over to Aunt Maggie's now."

Kayla walked so she'd have a chance to sort out her thoughts. It was hard to know what it would be like having Joey around, but seeing hope in her mother's eyes made it worth the chance.

Seeing Aunt Maggie in her work clothes with pieces of hay clinging to her hair was also a welcome sight. They hugged warmly. Finally, Aunt Maggie said, "Sundance has healed nicely. Any further developments with Olaf?"

Kayla spent the next half hour telling Aunt Maggie about confronting him when she was stuck in the driveway and after giving Daisy a ride on Sundance. When she told about the cigarette burn, Aunt Maggie said, "I know Daisy doesn't want the police called, but this is serious." Then Kayla told how she'd hoped Marta would be a support for Daisy until their trail ride that Saturday, the day the rock slide had almost bulldozed her and Sundance over the edge.

"Kayla!" Aunt Maggie's vivid green eyes widened. "Don't ever be alone with her again. I can't imagine why she'd do it, but I don't trust any of them. She could be as psycho as Olaf. Did you tell your folks?"

"No," Kayla said. "I can't upset them right now. They have so much on their minds. You know about Joey, don't you?"

"Yes. Both your mom and dad seem excited about it. I think they've decided to move forward. Not that Ned will ever be forgotten or replaced, but they could give Joey so much love, and my guess is Joey will help the healing process for your family. I sure hope so."

"With Joey's father dead, his mother in jail, and his grandma sick, do you—" Kayla paused to control her breathing, "—do you think Mom and Dad would ever want to try adopting him?"

"If they did, would you mind?"

Kayla tried picturing herself with Joey as a brother. Having a disturbed boy living in their house could be like having Nerad or Rottweiler living with them. They'd have to be constantly on guard, fearful, not knowing what to expect next. Joey would probably be slamming doors, picking fights, and arguing about doing his homework. Then again, there may be other moments they'd have together that she'd cherish. She shrugged. "It's too early to tell."

"Of course it is," Aunt Maggie said.

After walking inside the house and seeing her mother busy unpacking and Dad settled down with the paper, Kayla went into Ned's old room. She ran her hand over the maple headboard and straightened the green and burgundy striped comforter. She suddenly remembered that the brother her old boyfriend Luke had lost was also named Joey. Somehow that seemed significant.

What would it be like to have someone else's things in this room? she mused. *What would Joey be interested in? Would he like the outdoors? Camping? Turtle trapping?*

Fourth of July fireworks? Kayla found herself hoping he'd like them all and that she could share them with him.

It wasn't until the following day after lunch that she could discuss it with Rob. "Do you want to walk to Silent Rock?" he asked.

"Yes. I have lots to tell you." Once they were in their special valley surrounded by towering trees, rock cliffs and small waterfalls, Kayla told him what her parents had proposed. "I can't picture what it will be like having Joey around," she concluded.

"Well, picture a kid riding around on his bike, bringing home stray kittens, asking his big sister to take him horseback riding."

"Big sister," Kayla said.

Rob reached for her hand. "And it couldn't have come at a worse time. You have the worry of Daisy to say nothing of your own grandpa, and to top it all off, that perverted professor."

During the rest of the day, Kayla's thoughts strayed from Daisy to Grandpa to Dr. Nerad to Joey and back again. *Does Joey miss his mother?* Kayla wondered. She tried to imagine herself as Joey, staying in a temporary foster home, not having a place to belong. *What would it be like having a mother who cared more about her drug habit and boyfriends than about me?*

What had the Native American speaker said? Honor the Earth Spirit and take care of its land and its people. A first step in helping Joey would be to get to know him better.

That evening Kayla asked her mom, "Should we invite Joey to come out to the farm? Maybe he'd want to ride Sundance."

Mom looked at her gratefully, making Kayla wish she'd said something sooner. "I bet he'd like that. I've told him all about the horses. I'll call the Coopers right now." She headed for the phone, then turned back, "When would be good for you?"

"How about the morning of the first Monday of spring break? I'll have more time then."

A few minutes later Mom's voice cracked with excitement. "The Coopers' said April fifth would be fine. Mrs. Cooper plans on scheduling a perm that day and will drop him off for a while." She gave Kayla a quick hug. "Thanks, honey."

The phone rang again, and Kayla was sure it was the Coopers telling them Joey didn't want to come. But Mom's smile grew even bigger. "It's Grandma," she announced joyously, "Grandpa came out of the coma. He's doing remarkably well."

Kayla clasped her hands. "I have to call Rob."

After sharing the good news, she sighed. "I wish I could see Grandpa." Her gaze rested on the Ho-chunk basket. "But I'm happy that my first dream came true, and maybe by tomorrow when I get my research paper back, my second one will, too."

○ ○ ○

The next morning Kayla left early, hoping the books she'd ordered about sexual harassment were in. They were and she skimmed through them. One said to be assertive without attacking or being aggressive; to state with authority and confidence that you will not tolerate being treated in this manner. Could she do it?

Kayla set aside the reading. If she couldn't and had to file a complaint, it would be awful. Picturing the humiliated faces of Mom and Dad made her cringe. In a small town like Loomis, everyone would whisper about it, stating their opinions as to who's right and exaggerating every rumor. Kayla could almost hear a lady at church saying "That Kayla Montgomery always did like teasing the boys. Why, when she was in Sunday School, she couldn't leave poor Austin Anderson alone." The lady wouldn't mention how Austin had poked, made faces, and teased.

Mrs. Nerad would be devastated, too, Kayla guessed. She'd probably hate Kayla, blaming her for causing such turmoil in their lives. There would also be fellow professors who might side with their coworker. Some would treat her differently, possibly not wanting to confer with her alone or watching every word they said for fear she'd file against them. Lives would be permanently altered. The cost would be tremendous.

Ten minutes before history class, she reviewed her plan of action. Taking several deep breaths, she headed to class.

Outside the door, Kayla lost her confidence and broke into a sweat. On rubber-band knees, she entered the room. Nerad began by announcing, "I've graded your papers." Kayla's mouth turned instantly dry and she fought not to cough. He continued, "I'll return them after class."

Kayla forced herself to concentrate and take notes on the Industrial Revolution lecture. Afterwards, Nerad called out students' names and handed them their papers. Finally, Kayla was the only one still remaining. When the room was empty, he set her research paper down. He didn't seem the least bit hurried and his eyes roamed from her face to her legs, then back up again. She wished he would hand her her paper so she knew what she was dealing with. He was still taking in her conservative navy blue dress pants and cable knit sweater when he smiled. "You look like you're applying for the ol' school marm job."

"I wanted to talk to you about that," she said. Kayla hadn't intended on starting the conversation this way, but she plunged ahead.

"Shall we go to my office?" he asked. "It's a bit more private."

"No," she said, looking him square in the eyes, "I'd like to talk here." Without letting him say another word she continued. "After our last conversation I'd feel uncomfortable working with you on that project, and you'll need to find someone else."

"Oh? You aren't afraid of me, are you?" Kayla's heart thumped wildly, but her instincts advised her not to let him know.

"No," Kayla said.

"I'd like us to be friends, Kayla." His face went soft, like raw bread dough. "Share ourselves with one another, completely."

Kayla had rehearsed a similar scene in her mind and now in a confident voice said, "Dr. Nerad, I'm not interested in sharing my life with you. I'm here to discuss my class work. Nothing else."

"All right," he said, his back stiffening and eyes narrowing. "Let's discuss your paper. I read it and have to say I see some major problems. You chose to write on the family structure and how a woman's place has changed over the centuries. Yet you never discussed what a mother's role was supposed to be or why. You needed to explain how women reacted to these expectations, then compare it to modern times." Kayla's mouth dropped open. "Also, for a research paper, you have entirely too much of your own opinion without supportive detail. For example," he read off her paper, "'Many people have the mistaken opinion that women in the 1800's were compliant, subservient, or docile. They forget about Susan B. Anthony, Lucretia Mott and Elizabeth Cady Stanton.'" He stared her down. "You leave it at that, never explaining what these women did."

"Dr. Nerad," Kayla said recovering slightly, "the paper was already ten pages and you asked us to keep it under ten."

He shook his head. "I specified I wanted supportive details to substantiate all major points." He studied her face. Kayla set her jaw. Nerad stared her down. "At this point, I'd have to grade this paper a D."

"May I see the paper?" Kayla asked in a calm, determined voice which hid her true feelings.

Nerad retrieved it from his desk. There wasn't a single mark on it. *Had he been prepared to give it an A if I'd been compliant?* "Now," he said in a sick, sultry voice, "I'd be willing to take another look if you made a few changes." He brushed her hand with his. "Or maybe we could work on it together."

She withdrew her hand and looked him squarely in the eye. "I'm not interested in working with you. I find your comments and behavior inappropriate. You are my professor and your innuendoes are disturbing. You will stop and you will grade my work fairly or I will go to the dean."

"Are you threatening me?"

"Call it what you like, Dr. Nerad. Grade this paper fairly or I'll leave here and head straight to the dean's office to file sexual harassment charges."

Nerad's face hardened, but he said nothing.

"They'll investigate your past and possibly discover the true reason you left Cornell." It had only been a guess, but Kayla noticed his squinty eyes twitch. He recovered quickly, however.

"You don't have a leg to stand on," Nerad said with bravado, "it's your word against mine." Still, she thought she detected a note of panic in his voice. She charged ahead.

"We'll see about that." She handed him the paper.

He sat down at his desk. "You start spreading lies about me and...and you'll regret it." Nerad's words, though, had lost their punch. He seemed to be considering the consequences and his shoulders slumped.

Kayla leaned over and said, "I'll make you a little deal. I won't spread this around unless..." she paused until he looked up at her... "unless I hear complaints from other young women. And I'll be listening for them. If that happens, I'll go public."

Nerad looked at Kayla's paper for a long time. Finally, he picked up a pen and wrote a B on the top. Kayla thought she heard voices from the past. *Susan's? Lucretia's? Elizabeth's?* She left the office with their applause ringing in her ears.

○ ○ ○

Kayla had done it! She'd stood up to Nerad and made him back down. Time to celebrate with a spaghetti supper for her parents and Rob, she decided, and began the preparations.

Awhile later, as she filled goblets, Mom and Dad raised eyebrows. And when Rob made a toast, "To the tigress, Kayla Montgomery," Mom and Dad raised their eyebrows even higher. She would tell them the story—someday.

As she took a sip of the sparkling grape juice, though, she felt guilty about celebrating when a fellow victim was still in danger. She hadn't seen Daisy for two weeks. She had no idea how Daisy was doing, if her burn was healed or if she now had any other signs of abuse. If only she could talk to Daisy, she'd tell her about her experience with Nerad and how it was possible to stand up against an aggressor. Maybe with Kayla's coaching, Daisy'd be able to ward off future abuse.

Tomorrow will be Thursday. Will Rottweiler have let down his guard and returned to his bi-weekly suppers with his trapping buddies? She'd stop out to The Corner Cafe and see.

○ ○ ○

As soon as Kayla got back from classes on the following afternoon, her parents left for a session with the counselor. Kayla imagined they'd talk about how it felt to have Joey stay in Ned's room and whether including Joey in family activities would help them in the grieving process. Kayla was getting ready to go to The Corner Cafe when the phone rang.

"Is this 293-4343?"

Daisy! Kayla clutched the phone. "Yes, Daisy, it's Kayla. Are you all right?"

"No! Olaf tried to poison me."

"Poison you? Is he there now?" Kayla glanced at the clock. Four-fifteen.

"No, he left for the cafe. Please come over."

"I think I better call the police—"

"No!" Daisy shrilled. "Don't call the police. If he finds out the police were here, he'll kill me. He'll hide my body where it can never be found."

"Calm down now, Daisy. How do you know he tried to poison you?"

"My food tasted funny—sour." Her voice rose to a screech. "He's trying to kill me. Please help me. Take me away from here."

"All right, just calm down. I'm coming over." As she started her car, she fervently hoped Daisy had exaggerated. If she hadn't, Kayla's conscience would force her to take the old woman home with her. And any man who would report Todd Gillespie for taking his traps would surely hang her for taking his wife.

Kayla realized after pulling into the Erickson's driveway that she hadn't left a note for her parents. *Too late now!*

Daisy was watching from the window. As soon as Kayla entered the house, she could smell baked chicken. "Oh, hello, Kayla." Daisy's eyes were glazed and Kayla wasn't sure the woman remembered calling her. *Is her confusion due to poisoned food or was she being drugged?*

A plate of food sat at the table. The chicken was covered with a white sauce and mushrooms. A portion of broccoli looked half-eaten. Daisy's eyes focused. "That's the food Olaf wants me to eat, but I know what he's up to. He's poisoned it. Taste it! Go ahead and taste it."

Kayla wasn't keen on doing that. Instead she picked it up and smelled it. "M-mmm, cooking sherry and sour cream. Do you think you're just not used to those flavors?"

"I'm not eating that," she said.

"I'll dump it then and fix you something else." She went into the kitchen and Daisy followed. The kitchen entrance was too narrow for the wheelchair though, and Daisy had to stay outside. *Too narrow!* Kayla suddenly realized Daisy wouldn't have been able to take a casserole out of the oven. Marta had lied!

"Daisy," Kayla said, "how's your burn and bruise?"

Daisy pushed up her sleeve and Kayla happily discovered that both had healed. Yet to be sure, she had to ask. "Have… " Kayla fumbled trying to find the right words, "have there been any other incidents?"

Cr-eak! The noise made her jump. *Is Rottweiler home?* Kayla held her breath, waiting for the front door to swing open. When it didn't, she quickly restated the question. "You haven't been hurt anywhere else, have you?" Daisy wrung her hands, then wrapped herself tighter in her coat. Her dead-fish eyes stared at Kayla. Then they focused. Blood hammered in Kayla's ears, trying to block out the dreaded words she was certain she'd hear. Daisy's voice slid up a whole octave and her words rushed like someone longing for escape. "Someone took it! Someone took my tortoise-shell mirror!" Her eyes were frantic. "They hid it in the steam room. I know they did. Would you get it for me?"

The look of confusion and panic on Daisy's face made Kayla go to her. She patted her arm and said, "It's all right, Daisy." Kayla knew then that she needed to call someone. The police or Marta. Daisy needed help.

"Daisy," Kayla said calmly, "did Mr. Erickson give you any pills before he left?" If Rottweiler had given her hallucinating drugs, they'd still be in her system. The police could order tests be taken. But why would Rottweiler do that? It didn't make sense for him to want her to be like this.

"Go check," she pleaded. "I want my mirror. Please, go check."

"All right," Kayla said, "but then I'd like to use your phone." She walked ahead of Daisy to the steam room. As she unbolted the door, her lip trembled. She told herself it was silly to panic. The thing wasn't on. She opened the door. "Daisy, there's nothing in here."

"Yes, there is. It's back by the pipe. Please look."

Kayla took a calming breath, then walked over by the pipe.

"See, Daisy, nothing—" With a bang, the door closed. The sound Kayla heard next made her heart freeze. The deadbolt clicked into place.

CHAPTER 10

Wolves in Sheep's Clothing

The hiss of steam hit Kayla like a dragon's scorching breath and she couldn't hear anything further. In seconds, moist, hot air filled the room, saturating Kayla's clothes, hair, and skin.

"Daisy," Kayla pleaded, beating on the door. "Unlock the bolt. Please open the door."

No answer.

"Daisy, we'll look together for your mirror. Can you hear me? Open up."

Was she even still there?

Marta's warning words came back to her now: There's a lot you don't know about my mother. *Was it possible? Had Marta and Rottweiler been falsely accused? But the burn and bruise mark? Unless—had Daisy caused them herself? Beware of false prophets, which come to you in sheep's clothing, but inwardly are like ravenous wolves.*

Daisy might not intentionally be a wolf, but she was just as dangerous. Did she even realize the terror she was causing Kayla? What an idiot Kayla had been not to see. She should have learned from Nerad. People aren't always what they seem. The magnitude of her mistake overwhelmed her.

"Oh God, help me," she moaned. The steam was pouring out now. It was hard to see and the temperature was rising. Marta had said there was a malfunction in the thermostat. She grabbed the door handle again and turned with all her might, but it didn't budge. She banged on the door and screamed, "Daisy, open up." But Kayla was certain she was gone. Sweat dripped into her eyes and she wiped her face.

I can survive this, Kayla chanted to herself. *Breathe, just keep breathing.* The short gasps made her dizzy and she forced herself to draw in a full breath. *Fire.* Her lungs burned. Head whirling, she struggled to take off her sweatshirt. A clear thought tumbled into her head. *If I hold the sweatshirt against the pipe, the steam will stop coming out!*

Just take five steps toward the pipe and hold it against the end. That's all I have to do, she told herself. Sweat dripping from her face and falling into her eyes, she held the sweatshirt over her head like a shield as she stepped toward the pipe. She didn't need to see it to feel its fury. The fire-breathing dragon spewed scalding steam.

Get to the pipe and she could stop it. Get out of the tub was the mantra she'd shouted to herself when the scalding water poured out at her. Hot water. In the tub. When she was little. Her mind fragmented and that day came roaring back.

Her small hands tried to shut off the hot water, but the knob was too hot. *Get out. Got to climb out.* She stood up quickly, but slipped and fell in face first. Bubbles and water. *Can't breath.* She sat up and screamed. She hit the water, hating the water, the scalding water that wouldn't let her breathe. *Mommy!*

Climb out. I have to get out! Too slippery. Mommy! Mommy!

Kayla collapsed on the tile floor, slipping into timelessness. Her body became a hard shell and she willed her mind to escape. She imagined going out owling with Rob again. *Remember how cool and wintry it was that night? Snow, cool snow. Then the—No,* she wouldn't think of the hot tub. But it was too late. Reality blazed its way back again, burning the inside of her nose with each breath. She breathed in panicked gasps. *If only I left my parents a note telling them where I was going.* She had no idea how much time had passed. How much longer could she stay alive in here? How much longer could she stay sane? She was so thirsty. *Incredibly thirsty.*

She looked at the pipe again. She could do it. Face shielded by the sweatshirt, she clenched her jaw, then took two running steps toward the steam. *Now!* She covered the monster's mouth, but the sweatshirt became instantly saturated and her hands burned from the heat. "Awww!" She retreated into the farthest corner and sank to the floor. "Help me, God," she pleaded. Her heart jammed at the back of her raw, strained voice. "Help me."

She closed her eyes. A pulsing wave of dizziness. Eyelids tight and hot. *No escaping the steam. Steam everywhere. Mom, Dad, Rob. So unfair. Hot. Too hot.* She closed her eyes. Red and purple and black dots pulsated. She imagined someone opening the door, dragging her out, out into the cool air, into paradise.

Hands, big hands, hands pulling her out, thumping on her back. Coughing. Water pouring out of her mouth. Crying! Mommy's arms. Mommy holding me and crying. Holding me tight and crying.

She opened her eyes. Rottweiler! He was making her drink water. *Water! Lovely, cool water! More! More! Ice bags. Wonderful chilling ice. M-mmm, so good. So good.* She drank again and then, mercifully, exhausted, closed her eyes and slept.

When she awoke, Officer Finley and a woman with red hair were bent over her. "Kayla, wake up," Officer Finley said.

"Kayla, how are you feeling?" the woman asked, clipping something on her ear. "I'm going to take your temperature. Do you know where you are? Do you know what happened?"

"I... I...." She looked over at Daisy. Daisy must have remembered where she put the mirror. She was holding it with shaky hands, looking at herself with a pained expression. "Yes, I know." A chill went through Kayla as she saw those unfocused eyes. Daisy didn't even realize what she'd almost done.

Mr. Erickson came around in front of his wife, bent down and buttoned the top button of her coat. Daisy peered up at him. The look that passed between would be ingrained in Kayla's memory forever. It spoke of a lifetime together, of loving times, of hard times, of memories only they had shared.

Mr. Erickson tenderly fastened the second button, then the third and fourth. Daisy never stopped looking up at him. His lip trembled. Daisy's eyes misted. It was as if they knew they'd be separated and this was their one last moment together as husband and wife in their own home.

The paramedic interrupted the moment. "Kayla, your body temperature has come down within a safe zone, but it was quite high. The option is yours. Do you want to go to the hospital?"

"No, I'll rest better at home." Kayla turned for one final look at Mr. Erickson. His face had hardened once again, a protective shell covering his true feelings. Yet there had been genuine love there before. She was sure of that.

◯ ◯ ◯

After Kayla lay between her own cool sheets, Officer Finley's voice mingled with her parents', but she was too tired to listen. With the image of Mr. Erickson tenderly buttoning Daisy's coat, she fell asleep again.

Hot, so hot. She threw off the sheet. *Dragon! A fire-spitting dragon.* "Daisy!"

Mom was instantly at her side. "It's all right, honey. You're having a nightmare. It's over. You're safe." Kayla again lay down and almost instantly fell back asleep.

When she awoke, her clock said 7:09. She'd slept until morning. Her mom lay on a sleeping bag beside her bed. Kayla asked, "Did you sleep here all night?"

"We took turns," Mom said.

Rob and Dad, hearing voices, appeared. Rob stroked Kayla's face. "How are you?"

"I'm feeling much better."

"Hungry?" Dad asked.

"Yes," Kayla said sitting up. "Actually, I'm starved."

While Rob and Dad joyously cooked breakfast, Mom helped Kayla dress. "No hot shower this morning," Kayla said, trying out a joke.

While Mom brushed Kayla's hair, she said, "I've never forgiven myself for taking my eye off you when you fell into that bathtub. I couldn't stop thinking about that last night."

"Don't feel guilty about that, Mom. Accidents happen."

Mom hugged her, and Kayla hugged her back. Kayla knew when they felt she was up to it, there'd be a long lecture about being more cautious. And she'd have to agree that she'd made some poor choices.

Kayla said, "You're a wonderful mom."

"Well," Mom said after giving her a kiss, "this wonderful mom is going to help with breakfast. It smells like the men have pancakes for you."

Kayla had just taken her first bite when there was a knock on the door. "I better whip up some more batter," Dad joked, walking over to greet Officer Finley.

Kayla rose.

"It's good to see you up and about," Officer Finley said to her.

"It's great to be here."

"Please have a seat," Mom said. "We're starting some more pancakes."

"Well, all right."

"Is there news?" Dad asked.

"Yes. Mr. Erickson agreed to have Daisy signed in to Tri-County Nursing Home. He admitted that he'd been trying to have her stay at home as long as possible, but his nerves were packed tight and raw and he wasn't able to handle her anymore."

"What's wrong with her?" Kayla asked.

"She suffers from Alzheimers. It's been getting worse and she's become incontinent. The fact she locked the door on you shows all the more that it isn't safe for her to be unattended. I doubt she meant to hurt you. She's very confused and she probably forgot the incident a second after shutting the door."

All the calling and pounding, Kayla mused. *She probably never heard or understood.*

Officer Finley said, "Mr. Erickson is cooperating, and I must say I've enjoyed our conversations. There's a lot more to the man once he opens up." He rubbed his chin. "It may be that he was so unfriendly because he wanted to keep people away so they wouldn't find out about Daisy's growing problems." The officer accepted a cup of coffee. "The strain added to his poor attitude, too. His daughter said without his trapping buddies and their twice-a-week get togethers, he would have gone off the deep end." Kayla didn't doubt that was true. She knew he felt guilty for leaving Daisy alone, and that their time left together was growing short.

"And Daisy's bruise and burn mark?" Kayla asked. "Have they questioned Mr. Erickson or Marta about them?"

"Yes. They were due to Daisy's clumsiness and forgetfulness, which is now becoming more frequent. The bruise was from a lamp falling on her and the burn from her forgetting she had a lit cigarette. If she forgets a cigarette somewhere in the house, she could burn it down." He shook his head. "I wonder if, in her worsening state of confusion, she really thinks Olaf caused them. More likely, because she can't remember, she covers up her confusion by blaming him."

"She might not know she's lying, but Marta surely does." Kayla narrowed her eyes. "Marta told me Daisy had accidentally gotten the burn while spilling a hot casserole she was taking out of the oven. Why didn't she tell me the truth?"

Officer Finley shrugged. "She was probably covering for her parents. She knew her dad wanted to keep her mom at home as long as possible, and she was helping him do that. She wanted me to tell you how sorry she is for what happened."

Kayla rested her head in her hands. She had a little apologizing to do herself, she realized. The rock slide must have been a legitimate accident after all.

Officer Finley finished, then excused himself. "I'll keep in touch," he said.

After he left, Kayla said to her parents, "You two better get to work. You've missed so much already. I'll clean up here, then I'm going to get ready."

"Ready for what?" Mom asked.

"Work and classes."

"You were nearly hospitalized, Kayla." Mom turned to Rob. "Talk to her, will you?"

After they left, Rob asked, "Why push yourself? Take the day off."

"I'd be tempted," Kayla said, "except that if I'm not in Nerad's class, he might think he's intimidated me. And that's the last thing I want him to think."

○ ○ ○

Dr. Nerad glanced up briefly as Kayla walked in. She participated in the discussions and he treated her like the others. When he mentioned that parts of today's lecture would be on the final exam, his eyes flickered at Kayla.

He backed off quickly, though, and Kayla knew the mole was headed back underground.

Five days later, the Monday after Easter and the first official day of spring break, Kayla felt fully recovered; confident and relaxed. Daisy was being cared for at Tri-County and the nurses felt she was ready for visitors. Having someone around constantly who understood Alzheimers had made a huge difference. Kayla shopped for Rob's anniversary gift, and after taking a second look at the turkey sculpture, she bought it. Then she headed to the barn.

She had just one stall left to clean when Mrs. Cooper dropped off Joey. His foster mother took off so fast in her car, Kayla wondered if she intended to come back. Joey scuffed down the driveway toward her. He seemed smaller and more wiry than last time she'd seen him. His hair was the same: unkempt, falling in his eyes, his eyes a turbulent brown that reminded Kayla of the water at the end of the falls where it collided with the rocks. Those eyes narrowed now. *Oh, boy,* Kayla thought, *he's not going to make this easy.*

"I didn't want to come. All-pro wrestling's on."

Kayla gritted her teeth, but asked, "You like wrestling?"

"Yeah, my gramma likes it, too. When she's better I get to go back and live with her."

Kayla nodded. Joey quickly wiped his eye. *Was that a tear?* Hands in his pocket, Joey sauntered toward the horse trailer and Kayla followed. She imagined he worried about what would happen to him if his grandma died. The thought of having to live with his mom must have been almost as bad as the thought of not being able to live with her. Confusion, uncertainty, fear, separation. He must feel a combination of these emotions nearly all the time.

"Say," Kayla said after he'd finished looking over the trailer and turned toward the barn, "want to help me?"

He shrugged his shoulders, but followed her inside. "What'ja need?"

"To finish these stalls."

"I don't shovel no manure."

Kayla didn't respond, just walked into the barn and started shoveling.

After a few minutes, Joey followed her. "Mrs. Montgomery said you have a horse out here."

"Yes, come and see her." Kayla set down the shovel and led him out to the pasture. "See that gorgeous Saddlebred? That's Sundance."

"Your own horse?"

"Uh-huh."

"You get to ride her whenever you want?"

"I do. Would you like to ride her?"

"You mean today?"

"Sure."

"Maybe next time." His eyes widened and he threw out his chest. "I got a pair of cowboy boots. They're too small, but I bet I could still get in them."

"Okay," Kayla said, "next time then." They were building a history, she realized.

Joey asked, "You got to do all the chores around this place?"

"Not all. My aunt and uncle do most. Today they're letting me grain the horses, though." As she filled the food boxes, she asked, "Have you ever lived on a farm?"

"Yeah, once, in Texas, but we didn't have any animals. My mom's boyfriend had a pit bull, though."

Kayla wondered what they'd be like for a pet. She knew it would depend on how they'd been trained, just as it had with Mr. Erickson's Rottweilers. Both could probably be wonderful pets with proper handling.

"You'll want to stand back," Kayla warned. She opened the gate and the horses hurried through. Taffy took a wrong turn and ended up in Licorice Whip's stall. Kayla said, "Get out of there, Taffy." Taffy saw Licorice Whip coming, and quickly departed for the only remaining empty stall.

Joey's eyes were big again. "They all know where to go?"

"Uh-huh."

"They're pretty smart. Could I brush your horse?"

"Sure, you're probably tall enough."

Joey threw back his shoulders and straightened. As he brushed Sundance, reaching as high as possible on her neck, Kayla studied him. Scruffy, scowling, but there was something more there, too. His eyebrows were furrowed as he concentrated, brushing with just the right touch, not too hard or soft. He paused and ran his hand along Sundance's shoulder. It reminded her of something. *That's it! Ned and his hamster, Tiny Tim.*

Ned had loved the tawny-colored hamster and when he died, he'd been heart-broken. The ground was already frozen so her father had put him in the basement freezer, explaining that they'd bury him in the spring. The next day Kayla had gone into the basement and noticed the freezer, light on. Approaching, her mouth dropped open and stayed open. Ned was holding and petting the frozen hamster. He had petted Tiny Tim as tenderly as Joey was stroking Sundance now.

Soon after finding Ned with Tiny Tim, Kayla had gone with him to the pet shop. She'd explained that she knew Tiny Tim couldn't be replaced, but she was also sure there was a pet out there who would like being a part of their family. Ned had picked out a small aquarium and goldfish. At first Kayla didn't think a fish would ever substitute for a pet he could hold, but she was wrong. Ned enjoyed them in a different way. She wondered if the same would happen with her and Joey.

Joey: scruffy, loud, ill-mannered Joey. At first impression, there was no hope for him. Snap decisions could be deceiving, though. She'd found that out from Dr.

Nerad, whose accolades had impressed her when her instincts should have had her running in the opposite direction. Daisy and her family had also fooled her. They each had something hidden under the surface which was only revealed after Kayla got to know them. Wolves in sheep's clothing; sheep in wolves' clothing.

As Joey returned the brush to the tack room, she stole another glance. Joey was a boy with problems, but a boy with sensitivity and gentleness as well.

○ ○ ○

Later that evening, dressed in her new yellow dress, Kayla joined Rob, Mom and Dad. She looked around her, feeling a great outpouring of love. *Could there be room for one more? Yes,* she thought, *there could be.*

Aunt Maggie called asking if they wanted to see the pictures Uncle Jim had gotten back from Russia. "Sure," Mom said.

"Maybe another time," Rob said, squeezing Kayla around the middle.

"I guess these two want to be alone," Mom teased.

After they left, Rob kissed her and said, "Your mom is a smart lady."

Kayla teased, "You're just being romantic because you know I have an anniversary present for you."

"That must be it," he said. "I have something for you, too." He returned with a large white, decorated envelope.

He'd used shiny paper, fabric, and torn paper to create a scene on the front.

"This is the first time I'll be framing the wrapping paper," she said, admiring the metallic sun setting over calm water. Two figures were walking hand in hand along a white beach. "This is beautiful."

"Guess what's inside." Rob leaned toward her.

Kayla shook it. "Since it's a beach scene, maybe tickets to see the play *Hawaii?*"

"Nope."

"Hmmm." She held it up to the light. "It couldn't be something to wear—unless…" She smiled. "You didn't get me a bikini, did you?"

He laughed. "Darn, I missed my chance. I should have thought of that."

She looked carefully at the envelope and noticed three little crabs near shore. Rob had even added their claw tracks and escape holes. They were hard to see at first, but now she clearly distinguished them as the ghost crabs that blend in with the sand at Alabama. "Something to do with Alabama?" she asked.

"Open it."

Kayla unfastened it carefully so she wouldn't ruin the art work. She pulled out two tickets. "Airline tickets! To see Grandpa?"

"Yes. I thought you and I could fly there tomorrow, stay for the rest of our spring break, see your grandparents and take in the country. I want to catch me one of those ghost crabs."

Kayla sat up straight. "How perfect! Grandma and Grandpa will love meeting you. I can show you the bird sanctuary, and we can soak up some sun, walk the beach—"

"And crash the waves?"

"You bet! This is going to be great."

"Now it's your turn." She handed him his present. "First, though, you have to answer a question."

"Ask away," Rob said.

"Do you remember the first day we met?"

"Of course." His mischievous smile showed he did. "I was turkey hunting and your horse spooked a tom and ruined my shot."

Kayla laughed. "You said you would rather have had a camera anyway."

"That was just so I wouldn't scare off the beautiful spitfire of a girl I had already desperately fallen in love with."

"Desperately?"

His eyes softened. "Hopelessly and eternally."

"All right. You passed the test," she said smiling. "Go ahead and open it."

When Rob lifted the sculpture of the tom and hen turkey from its box, he was momentarily speechless. "This is excellent." He turned it around. "Oh, and look! There are chicks hidden in the back."

Kayla nodded. "I like it because I find something different, a deeper layer, every time I look at it." She ran her fingers over the sculpture. "It keeps revealing things the more time you spend with it." She added, "Like I hope to do with you."

Rob set down the statue and brought Kayla to her feet. He wrapped her in his arms and kissed her. "I love you," he finally whispered, holding her away so he could look at her. "And I want you in my life. One day I hope we'll talk about our future and plan it out together."

"I hope so, too."

He stroked her cheek and she wished the moment would last a lifetime. It was a buttoning-your-coat moment which spoke of love, commitment and caring. It was a beginning.

THE END